"Oh, I'm sor

As Holly stepped out of the elevator into
a world of her own, she found herself
in Jacques Querruel's arms, the file he
was holding spreading its pages over the
floor as he dropped it to steady them both.

He looked devastating. "I thought we
decided last night it was Jacques?" he asked,
still holding her.

Holly was mesmerized. "But that was away
from the office," she said weakly.

"And this is in the office, and I still wish you
to call me by my first name, *mademoiselle*."

"People might get the wrong idea," she
insisted.

"I am the boss, am I not? I can do whatever
I want."

It used to be just a nine-to-five job...
until she realized she was

Now it's an after-hours affair!

Getting to know him in the boardroom...
and the bedroom!

Coming soon:

The Boss's Secret Mistress
by Alison Fraser
#2378

His Boardroom Mistress
by Emma Darcy
#2380

Mistress by Agreement
by Helen Brooks
#2390

Helen Brooks

THE PARISIAN PLAYBOY

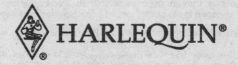

HARLEQUIN®

TORONTO • NEW YORK • LONDON
AMSTERDAM • PARIS • SYDNEY • HAMBURG
STOCKHOLM • ATHENS • TOKYO • MILAN • MADRID
PRAGUE • WARSAW • BUDAPEST • AUCKLAND

ISBN 0-373-12352-3

THE PARISIAN PLAYBOY

First North American Publication 2003.

Copyright © 2002 by Helen Brooks.

This edition published by arrangement with Harlequin Books S.A.

® and TM are trademarks of the publisher. Trademarks indicated with
® are registered in the United States Patent and Trademark Office, the
Canadian Trade Marks Office and in other countries.

Visit us at www.eHarlequin.com

Printed in U.S.A.

CHAPTER ONE

'AND how is the lovely Holly this morning? Had fun over the weekend, darling? You look like a girl who knows how to have a good time.'

As Holly raised her eyes from her word processor she steeled herself to show no reaction at all when she saw Jeff Roberts's podgy face leering at her from the doorway. 'Good morning, Mr Roberts,' she said flatly, her voice dismissive. And then she felt her stomach muscles contract as he sauntered over to her desk.

He was close enough now for his eye-wateringly pungent aftershave to invade her air space, but Holly continued typing without glancing at him again, hoping he would take the hint and leave.

There were basically three ways to deal with the problem of a serial groper in the office, Holly had decided some weeks before, when she had first started work at Querruel International.

One—ignore and avoid the sad individual in question, whilst letting him know by as icy a manner as possible that his advances were not appreciated.

Two—yell sexual harassment and take it as high as it needed.

Three—go for ultimate satisfaction and sock the scumbag a strong right hook on the jaw.

Holly had been trying the rational approach for eight weeks on the scumbag concerned with no visible result, and reporting him was a no-go unless she was prepared to lose her job because Jeff Roberts was the son of the managing director and the apple of his doting father's eye.

The third option would definitely mean she sacrificed all possibility of a future reference as well as the job—a job which had promised bright prospects and an interesting and rosy future at her initial interview. But—and the but had become increasingly attractive over the last couple of months—it would certainly teach the little wimp a lesson he wouldn't forget in a hurry.

He leant over her, reading the report she was copying from the draft on her desk, and his voice was low when he said, 'I've told you before, call me Jeff when there's just the two of us.'

There was always a faintly musty, almost unwashed odour emanating from his clothes, or maybe his skin, and Holly had to suppress a shudder of distaste. It didn't help that her tiny office was little more than a cubby-hole off Jeff's father's secretary's office, with one small window and wall-to-wall filing cabinets. There was one other door apart from that opening into the secretary's domain, and this would have led into the corridor outside but for the fact that two filing cabinets had been placed in front of it. Now necessity dictated one entered and left through the one door; something Jeff hadn't been slow to take advantage of from her first week.

'If you are looking for Margaret she should be back from the canteen in just a moment,' Holly said pointedly.

'Is that so?' As she continued with her work he adjusted his position, bending down and reaching across her for a pen and managing to brush the side of her breast as he did so. 'I'll just borrow this for a moment, if I may?'

Holly stopped typing, forcing herself to stare up into his sallow, moist face as she said steadily, 'I've told you before, Mr. Roberts, I don't want you to do that.'

'Do what?' He didn't even bother to try to sound indignant, and when his gaze moved over her breasts and then down to her legs before returning to her face his tongue wet his lower lip.

'I don't want you to touch me,' she spelt out tightly.

'Did I touch you?' He smiled, bending closer again and giving her the full benefit of his bad breath as he murmured, 'Why don't we go for a nice little drink after work, eh? I know just the place. You'd like that, wouldn't you?'

When hell froze over! 'I'm afraid I've got other plans,' Holly said stiffly.

'Tomorrow, then?' Speckled hazel eyes of a muddy hue slithered over her greedily. 'I'll buy you dinner too if you're a good girl. Can't say fairer than that.'

Where *was* this man coming from? What did it take to puncture this inflated ego that thought because of his standing in the firm he could behave however he liked? Holly knew from talk she'd heard in the canteen during her coffee breaks that Jeff Roberts pawed whomsoever he could, but most of the other girls worked in conditions where there was safety in numbers.

She stared him straight in the eye as she said coldly, 'I'm sorry but I can't go for a drink with you tomorrow or any other time, Mr. Roberts.'

His face changed. 'I can do you some good here, Holly, if you play your cards right,' he said very softly, 'but the opposite also applies. Do you understand what I'm saying?'

'I understand you very well,' Holly returned icily.

'And?'

'And my answer remains the same. Now, I need to get this report finished.'

He looked at her for a moment more before straightening up, and Holly was fooled into thinking he was going to leave as her eyes returned to her word processor. And then, for a shocking second, two meaty hands appeared over her shoulders and grabbed her breasts, squeezing them painfully hard before he went to walk away.

She didn't have to think about what to do. She was up out of her chair in the blink of an eye and all her strength was behind the ringing slap she delivered across his face.

He clearly hadn't expected anything like such a fiery reaction. He staggered backwards for a good few steps, thudding against a filing cabinet before letting forth with a string of obscenities which turned the air blue. As he straightened Holly knew he was going to come at her again and she prepared herself, her blue eyes flashing and her slim, petite body held stiff and tense.

'What the hell is happening here?'

The voice from the doorway brought Jeff swinging round and Holly's startled eyes focusing on the tall, dark figure standing in the aperture. She knew instantly who he was, even if the heavy French accent hadn't proclaimed it. She had heard so much from the other girls about the unique owner of Querruel International she could have described him down to the last eyelash, even though she'd never seen the ruggedly handsome Frenchman in person.

Jacques Querruel. Thirty-two years of age; unattached but with a string of mistresses and affairs that made him the favourite of society magazines and the tabloids, alike; the ultimate playboy except in Jacques Querruel's case he worked hard as well as playing hard. A self-made millionaire who had risen from the depths of squalor in a Paris slum to become a wealthy and successful industrialist, his original furniture company in Paris now having a string of subsidiaries in France as well as the United States and England.

And he played life by his own rules, as his present

ensemble proclaimed. According to office gossip he owned several flashy cars, as one would expect of a young French millionaire, but his favourite transport when he visited England was his Harley-Davidson.

'Mind-blowing piece of equipment,' one of the young lads in the accounts department had told Holly dreamily a couple of weeks ago. 'A Road King in monochrome black ice. You could really reel in the big miles on that beauty.'

'You ought to see Mr Querruel in his black leathers.' This had been from one of the females at the lunch table who clearly didn't want to waste time talking about a machine when it could be used discussing the rider. 'Everything stops when he walks in, I tell you. There's not a woman here who doesn't go weak at the knees. We're talking pure dynamite, Holly.'

And now she was seeing the pure dynamite for herself, Holly thought a trifle hysterically. And it was dangerous stuff all right. But then her attention was snapped away from the big black figure in the doorway and back to Jeff, when he said quickly, 'Mr Querruel, I'm sorry you had to be a party to this, sir. It's inexcusable, I know. I was reprimanding Miss Stanton on the inferior quality of some work she did for me and she reacted badly. I'm afraid I lost my temper when she hit me.'

'You liar!' Holly was amazed at his duplicity. 'How dare you—?'

'That's enough.' As her voice rose Jacques Querruel cut into her protest, his voice quiet but razor-sharp. 'We will discuss this in Mr Roberts's office, please. You will both accompany me there now.'

'Now, just hang on a minute!' Holly had thrown caution to the wind, she was so mad. She knew what would happen when Mr Roberts Senior got involved in this—

she'd be out on her ear quicker than you could say Harley-Davidson. 'He's lying. There was no work—'

'Have I not made myself clear?' The French accent was stronger than ever. 'We will discuss this matter in the privacy of Mr Roberts's office, Miss Stanton. I have already been informed that Mr Roberts is not expected back from a prior appointment for another hour, so we will not be interrupted.'

Had he guessed the reason for her objection? Holly stared into narrowed amber eyes that had all the softness of that solid fossilised resin, and found she couldn't drag herself away from the translucent gaze. They were unnerving, those eyes. Mesmerising and beautiful but cold, like the predatory surveillance of a wolf or one of the big cats.

And then she mentally shook herself, angry with the fanciful description. What on earth was the matter with her? she asked herself silently as she followed the two men through into Margaret's office, and then beyond into Mr Roberts Senior's large and opulent domain.

She just had time to notice Margaret standing against her desk, looking aghast, which implied the managing director's secretary had heard something of the events which had transpired in her coffee break, but then the door was firmly shut and she was alone with Jacques Querruel and a blustering Jeff Roberts. 'Really, Mr Querruel, there is no need for you to concern yourself with this unfortunate matter,' he was saying with ingratiating and sickening servility. 'You've obviously got more important things to do and—'

'On the contrary, Jeff.' It was cool, very cool, and as Jacques Querruel indicated for them both to be seated with an authoritative wave of his hand Jeff said nothing more.

Holly had expected the Frenchman to seat himself behind the massive oak desk which dominated the room, but instead he perched easily on the edge of it, the piercing eyes surveying her critically.

She forced herself not to fiddle with her hair or make any other nervous movement, but it was hard. Especially in the circumstances and with Jeff sitting a foot or so away. But there was absolutely no way she was going to give any ground over this. She raised her small chin at the thought, her eyes stormy.

'So…' Jacques's compelling gaze moved from her flushed face to Jeff's sulky one, and the amber eyes took full note of the unmistakable handprint etched on the other man's plump cheek. 'I think there is a problem, yes?'

'Nothing I can't handle, Mr Querruel—'

'Yes, there darn well is!' It was Holly's turn to cut across Jeff's voice and she did it vehemently. 'I have asked Mr Roberts to keep his hands to himself on several occasions and today was the last straw. The man's a pervert and I refuse to be mauled by him one more time.'

Dark eyebrows lifted and the carved lips twitched a little before Jacques said, 'Do not beat about the bush, Miss Stanton. Say what you feel.'

So he thought this was funny, did he? The flare of furious resentment in Holly's eyes turned the blue purple as she glared at the illustrious head of Querruel International, and in that moment she didn't care a jot who he was. She stood to her feet, her voice shaking with rage as she said, 'Thank you, Mr Querruel. That's exactly what I intend to do. Your managing director's son is a liar as well as a lech. There is nothing wrong with my work and far from reprimanding me he had taken his molesting of recent weeks to a new high. That was why I slapped his face and he was lucky to get off so lightly.'

'This I can see.' It was a quiet murmur.

It wasn't the moment to think that he had the sexiest voice she had ever heard, richly seductive in spite of the disparagement, Holly thought with a strong burst of self-disgust.

'That's all utter rubbish.' Jeff decided he'd been out of the conversation long enough and he glared up at her, spite prevalent in his voice as he said, 'The actual fact of the matter is that Miss Stanton is not up to the job for which she was employed but I felt sorry for her. I've given her endless chances over the last weeks and realised too late she had misconstrued my kindness as personal interest in her. When I had to make it clear I did not appreciate her flirting with me she suddenly went crazy. A woman scorned and all that.'

Jacques Querruel's steady gaze moved over the fat, greasy-haired individual sitting in front of him before re-turning to the lovely young woman standing in front of the desk. She had hair the colour of dark, rich chocolate, smoothly groomed into a shoulder-length bob, eyes as blue as cornflowers and the sort of cheekbones many a model would have killed for. And she was mad. Boy, was she mad. It was as likely she'd made up to the slug in the chair as the pope marrying. He smiled. 'Do I take it you refute Mr Roberts's explanation?' he asked silkily.

Her nostrils flared. 'Darn right I do.' He was aggressively good-looking, hard and chiselled with no sign of softness about him at all. Funny, but from the other woman's gossip she'd pictured him as more pretty-boy handsome than anything, especially when they'd gone on about the tan and the jet-black hair and wickedly thick eyelashes. He *had* got all those things, and the eyelashes were gorgeous enough to be utterly wasted on a man, but there was nothing remotely boyish about Jacques

Querruel. In fact she wouldn't have been surprised to learn he had been born six feet two and radiating power and authority. He couldn't ever have been a helpless baby or vulnerable little boy.

'It would appear we have something of a stalemate.' The piercing amber eyes looked from one face to the other. 'Have either of you proof of what you claim? I take it Miss Stanton's work bears evidence of her ineptitude?' he asked Jeff smoothly.

'She—er—I mean, by the time it's been corrected...it's eventually brought up to scratch,' the other man finished lamely.

'And you, Miss Stanton? You have witnesses to Mr Roberts's over-familiarity?' The dark eyebrows rose again.

'It's not over-familiarity,' Holly said tightly. 'It's downright groping of the most intimate kind, and he thinks he can get away with it because he's the managing director's son. All the girls avoid him when they can. And, no, I haven't got any witnesses—Mr Roberts has always made sure of that. Stuck in that little box out there I haven't exactly got a way of escape or a camera whirring to record his goings-on, have I? And if you are going to ask me if any of the others would come forward to back up what I say, I don't know. Possibly, if they want to continue working here, the answer would be no.'

'A somewhat jaundiced view, Miss Stanton,' he drawled, his accent making her name sound very different.

'No, merely realistic,' she snapped back quickly. She was not going to bow and scrape to this arrogant individual like everyone else; neither was she going to be intimidated into saying anything less than the truth. No doubt Mr Roberts Senior would produce half a dozen female staff to swear that Jeff was approaching sainthood, along with suggesting to Margaret that her new assistant wasn't *quite* on the ball, but she couldn't do anything about that. Whatever, her days at Querruel International were numbered, which was a shame. She had fought off some stiff competition to secure the job and for it to end like this…

'So you have no faith in company procedure for this kind of incident?' Jacques Querruel asked softly.

Holly raised her head, her glossy curtain of hair shimmering with the movement. His keen appraisal was making her feel isolated and insignificant but those feelings weren't new to her and she was adept at hiding them. She swallowed, aware of tension tightening her jaw, but her voice was firm and steady when she replied, 'I have only been in this company's employ for eight weeks so I cannot answer that in a general sense.' She paused. 'However, with regard to this particular incident, and taking into account the person involved—' she shot Jeff a glance of pure loathing '—I would say it would be very naïve of me to think justice would be done.'

'I see.' Twice in the last few minutes Jeff Roberts had gone to speak and twice a commanding hand had motioned him to silence. Now Jacques Querruel turned his gaze on the other man as he said even more softly, his voice cold behind the velvet tone, 'And you, Jeff. Do you think justice will be done?'

'I have every faith in company procedure,' Jeff said pompously.

How could a man like Michael Roberts, a man he had every respect for and who was damn good at his job, have a son like this? And moreover think the world of him too? Jacques stood up, hiding his irritation at the situation and himself as he did so. He had known some time ago that he didn't want Michael's son to be a permanent fixture in the company, but the man had seemed efficient enough and there had been no reason to suggest getting rid of him.

Jacques walked over to the massive plate-glass window, staring down into the busy London street below for a moment. He should have followed through on his gut instinct, had Jeff Roberts transferred over to the French office for a few months so he could see how Michael's son functioned away from his father's protective hand. Of course, he hadn't known about this other side of the man... His mouth twisted sardonically. And now he was paying for his procrastination.

He turned, his mind made up. 'Suspension on full pay for the time being, Jeff, while this matter is fully investigated.'

'But—'

'No buts.' The words were crisp and without expression. 'This is the policy, as you know.'

'But I thought...' Jeff's voice trailed away. And then he made the mistake of continuing, 'You can't think there's any truth in this girl's story? She's a typist, and I'm...' He stopped abruptly as Jacques looked straight at him, the Frenchman's eyes amber flares of light. 'I mean, my father—'

'Will appreciate the need for absolute integrity in a matter of this kind,' Jacques finished smoothly.

Holly knew her mouth was slightly agape just a second after the devastating gaze swung her way, and although she brought her lips quickly together she saw the acknowledgement of her amazement touch the hard mouth in a slight smile.

'Have you anything further to say for the moment, Miss Stanton?'

Had she? Lots, probably, but right now her brain was as scrambled as an omelette. She shook her head dumbly.

'Then perhaps you would like to go into your…little box and write out a full statement of exactly what you allege occurred today, along with any other incidents which are relevant. Dates and times as far as possible, please. Mr Roberts will be doing the same in here with me.' He reached over and pressed the buzzer on the desk as he finished speaking, and Margaret appeared immediately like a genie out of a bottle, indicating the managing director's secretary had been burning with curiosity.

'Coffee, please, Margaret,' Jacques said pleasantly as Holly began to walk out of the room. 'And a cup for Miss Stanton too, if you would be so kind? She will take hers in the little box.'

'I'm sorry, Mr Querruel?'

Holly left them to it, shutting the door behind her before she dived across Margaret's office and into hers. She sat down at her word processor, glancing about the small space and aware her heart was beating like a drum and tears born of reaction weren't too far away. She took several deep breaths, willing herself to keep calm. It *was* a little box. He might not have liked the terminology, but, nevertheless, that was what it was, she told herself militantly as she forced her mind away from the main trouble of the day and on to Jacques Querruel's last words.

Margaret appeared in the doorway a moment later and her homely, middle-aged face was a picture. 'So what's *happened*?' she whispered urgently, adding inconsequentially, 'I've ordered the coffee.'

Holly told her as quickly and concisely as she could whilst they both kept an ear cocked for any movement from Mr Roberts's office, and when she had finished the older woman amazed her by putting a comforting arm round her shoulders as she said, 'He's a nauseating little bug, Holly, and he's needed squashing for a long time.

I've never had any trouble with him, of course—'
Margaret had been happily married for three decades and
had two grown-up children '—but I know at least one girl
who's left rather than cause a fuss when he kept bothering
her. I've tried to speak to his father about it on a couple
of occasions but I met with a blank wall. Mr and Mrs
Roberts lost two children in a road accident before Jeff
was born the following year, so he's always been able to
do nothing wrong in their eyes.'

'Whatever happens, I'm not going to be the flavour of
the month with him, then, am I?' Holly commented
miserably.

'Oh, don't worry, it'll be all right,' Margaret said brac-
ingly, and then as one of the canteen staff entered her
own office with the coffee she gave Holly another reassuring pat on the shoulder before bustling away.

She had better start looking for another job right now,
tonight. Holly sat staring at the dingy grey filing cabinets
for a moment or two, and then, as Margaret came in with
her cup of coffee, began typing out her statement. Just her
luck to end up in a place where the company lech was
the son of the managing director!

She found she had to concentrate very hard on what
she was doing over the next hour or so. Not that she
couldn't remember all the details of the incidents over the
last weeks—she could. Even though some of the dates
escaped her. But it was more the fact that the image of
an aggressively masculine face kept getting between her
and the keys.

She checked everything twice before she printed the
pages out, and then once the report was in her hand she
checked it again. She hadn't elaborated or exaggerated
anything, she decided at last. She hadn't had to. The bare
facts were bad enough. Seeing it all in black and white

like this made her wonder why she'd waited so long to give Jeff his come-uppance! She loathed bullies, and he was one of the sickest kind.

'It is that bad, yes?'

Her head jerked up from the papers in her hand to see Jacques Querruel standing watching her. One dark eyebrow was quirked mockingly and there was a disturbing gleam in the amber eyes. He had taken off his leather biking jacket, she noticed dazedly, and the plain charcoal T-shirt he was wearing sat on broad, muscled shoulders. He must work out every day to have a physique like that.

She felt her heart thudding against her ribcage and it annoyed her, along with his air of relaxed authority. He'd be fully aware of the effect he had on women, she thought hotly, expecting every female from Margaret's age down to fall at his feet in worship. For a moment she just sat there, dry-mouthed and silent, but then his arrogance sent the adrenalin flowing fiercely. He might be the sacred head of Querruel International, and drop-dead gorgeous to boot, but he had absolutely no effect on her at all, she told herself vehemently. Added to which she had the distinct feeling she wouldn't be working here much longer anyway.

She straightened, aware of the hectic colour staining her cheeks but unable to do anything about it. 'Judge for yourself,' she said curtly, knowing it wasn't at all the way to speak to the ultimate kingpin but unable to help herself.

The smile had been wiped off his handsome face, Holly noted with some satisfaction as he walked over to her and took the papers she was holding out. And she didn't know why but she made very sure their fingers didn't touch.

She had hoped he would take the report back to his office and read it there, but instead he idly brushed some papers out of the way and perched on the side of her desk.

Her little cubby-hole had never been big by any standards, as she'd already made abundantly plain to him, but now it seemed to shrink away to nothing. He was so close she could smell the exclusive, subtle odour of his aftershave, and that, together with the leather trousers stretched tight over lean male thighs, was making her face burn in the most peculiar way.

She forced her eyes upwards a little, where they fell on to his hands. They were powerful, with long, strong fingers and short, clean fingernails. An artist's hands, or maybe a musician's... And then she caught the thoughts angrily. He was neither of those things, for goodness' sake, she told herself irritably. She knew from office gossip that he was a ruthless, hard and inexorable businessman, who gave no favours and asked for none. He liked fast cars and motorbikes, and even faster women—so she had heard—and was a millionaire many times over. Not exactly the type of man to sit painting watercolours!

The chiselled profile was frowning when she looked at his face, and he raked back his hair—as black as a raven's wing—a couple of times as he read. Even sitting quite still as he was now vitality radiated from him; she had never come across such a disturbing man before. It was probably quite unreasonable, because to date she had to admit he had been pretty fair in the circumstances, but she didn't think she liked Jacques Querruel one little bit.

He was on the last page of the statement; he'd obviously got to the bit she'd written about the incident that morning, and to her surprise she heard him swear softly under his breath. She didn't speak French but there was no doubting the content of the muttered expletives. He turned his head, his amber eyes meeting her blue, and his tone was almost an accusation when he said, 'Why the hell did you not do something about this before? You are not the type who cannot say boo to the goose.'

The fact that his perfect English had let him down just a fraction gave Holly a disproportionate amount of satisfaction as she said coldly, 'I was hoping to deal with it myself with the minimum of unpleasantness.'

'Then you have not succeeded.'

'That's hardly my fault, is it?' she snapped back angrily. Hateful man! He'd be blaming her for everything in a moment. 'I wanted to keep my job; that's not a crime.'

'Indeed it is not, Miss Stanton,' he agreed smoothly. 'I understand you have only been with Querruel International a few weeks?'

'Eight,' she clarified militantly. 'And if you say Mr Roberts has been with the company for a lot longer without anyone complaining before that's not because there haven't been grounds, I assure you.'

'I see.' He stared at her consideringly and she made herself stare back without flinching. 'I was not going to say that, Miss Stanton.' He lifted the hand holding her statement. 'I may keep this?' he enquired softly.

She nodded. 'Yes, it's finished.' Just as she was finished at Querruel International. It might take a week or a month or six months, but sooner or later Jeff's father would find an excuse to get rid of her, however this thing turned out. And she wouldn't want to continue working so close to him as his secretary's assistant now anyway. The job had gone sour.

Jacques Querruel stood up, and once more she found herself pinned by his gaze. 'For what it is worth, I despise the type of man who threatens a woman in this way,' he said quietly. 'I can assure you I will investigate this matter very thoroughly, Miss Stanton, and rest assured Jeff's position in this company will not affect the outcome.'

Oh, come on, who was he kidding? He flitted here, there and everywhere, but Jeff's father ran this place for Jacques Querruel, and people were hardly going to slate his son knowing once the big boss left they would have no protection against any comeback from daring to speak the truth.

Holly wasn't aware her face was speaking volumes, not until the big, dark man in front of her said softly, 'You do not believe this?'

'No,' she said, because there was no point in lying. 'At least, I believe you'll do your best to get to the truth, but you won't. You see, everyone likes Mr Roberts Senior as much as they dislike his son, and they know how much he and his wife think of him. Also...' She paused, wondering if she should go on.

'Yes, Miss Stanton?'

'You are not here most of the time,' she said baldly.

'Ah, this I see.' The beautiful eyes narrowed thoughtfully. 'Then my enquiries will have to be in confidence and no names mentioned to Jeff's father, apart from yours, of course.'

Oh, great, wonderful. The sacrificial lamb. Still, it was only what she had expected after all; it just grated doubly that he seemed so unconcerned.

'That's all right, then.' She tried, she really tried to keep the sarcasm to a minimum but she was so angry she could spit.

Like before, he read her mind perfectly. The firm, slightly stern mouth suddenly twisted with the nearest thing to genuine amusement she had seen in the last caustic hour or so.

'You are not in awe of me, Miss Stanton,' he said softly.

It was a statement, not a question, which was just as well because Holly was beyond speaking at that moment. He had leant forward as he'd spoken, both hands resting on the desk and his body close enough for the warmth and smell of him to surround her. She felt her senses quivering and was furious with herself for being so weak and trembly.

'And that is unusual,' he continued thoughtfully, almost as though he was speaking to himself now. 'I am surrounded by a whole host of sycophantic beings, Miss Stanton. It comes, as they say, with the territory. The people who really speak their mind to me I can count on one hand and I would not use all my fingers.'

She didn't know what to say and so she said nothing.

'This was a…novelty at first. Perhaps even satisfying, I am ashamed to admit, in the early days.'

He didn't look ashamed, Holly thought, and she had no doubt he loved every moment of the power he was able to command so effortlessly, especially where the fairer sex was concerned. She had seen men like him before, men who considered themselves nothing less than demi-gods with the ability to direct and control other people's lives. Admittedly none of the others had looked as good as Jacques Querruel, but that would have to have made him more puffed up in anything.

She became aware he was waiting for her to speak. She pulled herself together and said evenly, 'So it isn't satisfying now, Mr Querruel?'

He looked at her for a moment without speaking and she wondered if she had gone too far, even though her tone hadn't been openly acidic. And then he grinned. 'Occasionally,' he admitted softly. 'Yes, occasionally it serves a purpose.'

Oh, wow! Oh, wow, oh, wow, oh, *wow*. Where had all the natural arrogance gone? If the other girls thought he was dynamite normally he had just moved up to nuclear-missile potential.

Holly cleared her throat, thinking that if she had known this morning she was going to have such an amazing, one-in-a-million day she would have worn her new suit and given more attention to her hair and make-up. And then she suddenly realised where her thoughts were going and checked herself firmly. It wouldn't make any difference if she was covered from head to foot in Dior and diamonds. Jacques Querruel was as far removed from her orbit as the man in the moon! Not only that, he was a heartless so-and-so.

'Margaret tells me your work is more than acceptable,' Jacques continued after a moment. 'In fact, "excellent" is the word she used.'

Good old Margaret!

'How old are you, Miss Stanton?' he asked with a directness that took her by surprise.

'Twenty-five.' She frowned. 'Why?'

He liked that in this young woman, the candidness, but she was something of a paradox and he did not like that. He did not trust what he did not understand, and one of his strengths was that he could sum people up very swiftly. She appeared to be strong and determined, one could almost say aggressively so, and yet several times now he had seen something else behind those great blue eyes. She intrigued him, and it had been a long time since that had happened.

'Why?' He repeated the word and then didn't answer her question, saying instead, 'Have you ever considered working abroad, Miss Stanton, or are you bound to home shores by family or maybe a boyfriend?'

Holly blinked. What had that got to do with anything? She stared at him, wondering how they had arrived at this from his initial reading of her statement. He was watching her coolly and she envied his detachment as her nerve-ends began to prickle. Her wary expression seemed to amuse him. His amber eyes glinted and a faint cynical smile twisted his lips. 'Well?' he prompted lazily.

'I...I wouldn't be averse to travelling in the future,' she said carefully, hating the little stutter at the beginning of her words and warning herself to show no weakness before this man.

'And family commitment? Love commitments?'

His French accent gave the last two words a sexy intonation an English voice couldn't hope to compete with. Holly hoped the heat which had surged in her blood wasn't reflected in her face, but she had the nasty feeling she was a definite shade of pink. 'I live alone in rented accommodation, Mr Querruel,' she answered primly, 'and I have some good friends but not a special man-friend if that's what you mean.'

He surveyed her for a second more as he straightened and then he said quietly, 'Mr Roberts has already left the premises so you can relax. I have some business to deal with but I would like to see you again before you leave tonight, Miss Stanton. You will not forget this?'

She wanted to ask why. He had her statement, and there was nothing she was prepared to add or delete from it. But, in view of the way he had successfully deflected any unwanted questions to date, she didn't bother, inclining her head as she said, 'Of course not, Mr Querruel. In Mr Roberts's office?'

'Just so.'

And with that he was gone.

CHAPTER TWO

THE rest of the day was an anticlimax. Holly went to lunch as usual with Margaret, in the excellent canteen the firm boasted, but the other woman didn't mention the events of the morning at all and fielded any attempt Holly made to discuss them. Holly was left with the distinct impression Margaret had been warned not to talk about the matter by a higher source: perhaps by Jeff's father, who was now ensconced in his office with Jacques Querruel, or the tycoon himself.

The afternoon was spent typing a long and involved but boring report with one ear cocked towards the outer office. Although Holly was aware of Jeff's father leaving at some point after she and Margaret had returned from lunch, Mr Roberts Senior did not look in on her, for which she was grateful. Another confrontation was beyond her for the present.

There was the usual coming and going in Margaret's office, and once or twice Holly heard a female speaking in a hushed but excited tone—no doubt due to the occupant of the room beyond, Holly thought cynically—but she worked on undisturbed. Once the report was finished she printed three copies, as Margaret had requested, and clipped each of them together before placing them in three prepared folders.

And then she stretched tiredly, shutting her eyes for a moment as she raised her hands high above her head with a big sigh. She had tried not to think about the impending meeting with Jacques Querruel but now it was imminent. She didn't want to see him again. Not ever.

'Tired?'

Her eyes shot open and there he was, standing in the open doorway, but now dressed in a light grey suit that must have cost a mint of money. The jacket was unbuttoned, revealing an ivory shirt tucked into the flat waistband of his immaculate trousers. He was the epitome of the successful tycoon, from the top of his sleek, dark head to the tips of his handmade shoes. He looked even more sexy than he had done in the leathers.

Holly was horrified the last thought had slipped in and straightened hastily in her seat, flushing hotly.

'It is nearly five-thirty.' He didn't wait for her to speak. 'And I think our little chat could be conducted more comfortably over dinner, yes? Are you free tonight, Miss Stanton?'

'*What?*' She was hallucinating now, she had to be, because he couldn't possibly have said what she thought he'd just said.

'Dinner?' he said with a patience which bordered on the insulting. 'I take it you do eat dinner? I asked you if you were able to accompany me tonight.'

Holly's flush deepened. Either he was stark staring mad or she was.

'There is a job proposition I would like to put to you,' he continued smoothly, 'which will obviously need some discussion. I am hungry and I am thirsty, and a good bottle of cabernet sauvignon is calling. If you are free tonight I will run you home and you can change. I have a table booked for seven.'

She stared at him, utterly taken aback. And then the thought surfaced—who would he be taking to dinner if she refused? The table was already booked and Jacques

Querruel didn't look the type to eat alone. No doubt he had a little black book to deal with such an eventuality. She forced herself to say, and calmly, 'I don't understand, Mr Querruel. You said a job proposition?'

'Don't tell me that you were not thinking of looking for another position forthwith?' he said quietly.

Holly's jaw set. This was a catch-22 question and however she answered it she couldn't win. If she denied it he would assume she was lying. That much was clear. If she confirmed his suspicions she might well find herself leaving Querruel International sooner than she had expected. Jacques Querruel was the type of employer who demanded absolute loyalty.

'What gave you that idea?' Holly chose her words carefully.

'Nicely fielded, Miss Stanton,' he said gravely.

Impossible man! She glared at him and he smiled back, a cynical twist of his cleanly sculpted mouth. 'So…I will give you another ten minutes to finish off here and then we will call by your apartment, yes?' he asked, his black eyebrows rising with derisive amusement at her confusion.

Holly thought of all the reasons that made it imperative she say no to this ridiculous invitation. The man was dangerous—*lethal*, in fact, as an adversary. She'd heard stories about his ruthlessness that would make the straightest hair curl. And she had made a formal complaint against the son of Jacques Querruel's managing director here in England. At the very least her accusations were going to cost the company time and effort, and she just might have stirred up something of a hornets' nest. This man was wealthy and powerful, cold and arrogant. He was also devastatingly attractive and used to having any woman he wanted with a click of his well-manicured fingers. She hated to admit it to herself but he scared her half to death.

And—and here she inwardly berated herself for the shallowness of her thoughts—she had nothing suitable to wear for dinner with a multimillionaire, and her little bed-sit was not exactly the type of home Jacques Querruel would be used to.

So, in view of all that, why could she hear herself saying 'Thank you, Mr Querruel. I would be pleased to hear what you have to say over dinner?'

'Excellent.' His gaze ran over her for one more second and then he turned without another word and she was alone again.

For as long as it took for the door to Michael Roberts's office to close, anyway. Then Margaret was standing where Jacques had just stood, her eyebrows disappearing into her hair. 'I don't believe what I just heard,' she whispered, coming right into the room and standing by Holly's desk. 'I've worked for Mr Roberts for five years and I've seen females galore throw themselves at Mr Querruel, and he's never even *noticed*. He's a man who keeps work and play totally separate.'

'This *is* work.' Holly was embarrassed and hot. 'He said something about a job proposition. I think he suspected that I couldn't stay on after what happened this morning.'

'Did you feel that?' Margaret asked unhappily.

Holly nodded. 'I guess so,' she admitted. 'It would be too awkward with me working for you and you being Mr Roberts's secretary. You see that, don't you, Margaret?'

Margaret stared at the lovely young face in front of her, and now her motherly instincts came to the fore as she said softly, 'Holly, be careful, won't you? Jacques Querruel is renowned as a love-'em-and-leave-'em type, and normally his partners are selected from women who think like him, if you know what I mean. They're all beautiful and sophisticated and often holding high-powered jobs—real career women. They don't want the ties of hearth and home any more than he does.'

Now it was Holly's turn to stare at the other woman. 'Margaret, he's only asked me out to discuss some sort of work proposal,' she said in astonishment. 'I think he believed me about Jeff Roberts, although he never said so, and he's probably feeling he owes me some sort of alternative job, that's all.' She could hardly believe Margaret was suggesting anything else. Jacques Querruel and a typist? It was laughable.

Margaret sniffed a very worldly-wise and maternal sniff. 'Be that as it may,' she said grimly. 'You just remember what I've said, that's all.'

'He asked me in your hearing,' Holly pointed out reasonably. 'He wouldn't do that if he wasn't serious about a job, would he?'

Margaret just looked at her, her plump chin settled in her ample neck and her eyebrows raised in a way she didn't mean to be comical but which struck Holly so.

'I promise I'll be careful,' Holly said at last, biting back a smile. 'OK? And I'll tell you everything that transpires in the morning, although I'm sure you're worrying unnecessarily. But thanks anyway,' she added, reaching out a hand and patting the other woman's arm.

She received a warm smile in return. 'I know you think I'm a fussy old woman but, in spite of the fact we've only known each other a little while, I think of you as a friend,' Margaret said earnestly. 'And with you not having any family as such, I feel you're a bit…'

'Vulnerable?' Holly proffered.

Margaret nodded unhappily.

'Believe me, Margaret, vulnerable I'm not,' Holly said firmly. 'I learnt to look after myself from when I could toddle; I had to—no one else was going to. And, if nothing else, being pushed around by the establishment and having six foster homes before I was eighteen makes one resilient.'

'You're telling me you're tough?'

The tone was so disbelieving Holly laughed out loud. 'I'm not a push-over,' she qualified. 'And I haven't met a man yet who could soft-soap me into doing something I didn't want to do.'

'Ah, but you hadn't met Jacques Querruel before.' Margaret gave a wise-owl nod of her head just as the telephone in her office began to ring, causing her to bustle back into the other room.

Dear Margaret. Holly sat for a moment, nipping at her lower lip with small white teeth. It was true, they had hit it off right away at the interview for the job, which Margaret herself had conducted, and she had enjoyed working with the other woman the last weeks. She'd thought she was really set up here; with Margaret backing her there had been no reason why she couldn't have worked herself up to a prime position in a few years with a nice fat salary to boot. She wasn't afraid of hard work— in fact, she thrived on it—and with no home commitments she could work as late as she liked when necessity commanded.

Margaret's warning continued to whirl round in Holly's head as she tidied her desk and turned off the word processor. She locked the filing cabinets—her last job of the day—with the spare set of keys Margaret had given her in her first week at Querruel International, before walking through into the other room.

This office was spacious, as befitted the managing director's secretary, holding two easy chairs and a small coffee-table along with Margaret's huge L-shaped desk. In one corner a bookcase held a selection of Querruel International brochures and magazines where their furniture had been advertised, and in another stood two filing cabinets holding material of a confidential nature. It was as different from Holly's little cubby-hole as chalk from cheese.

Margaret was still talking on the telephone as Holly emerged, and in the same moment Jacques Querruel strode through the open doorway of the other office. 'Ready?' he asked abruptly, and as Holly nodded he took her arm, calling goodnight to Margaret as he whisked Holly out into the corridor, whereupon the lift doors opened immediately he touched the button.

They had never done that for her, Holly thought bemusedly. She normally had to wait for at least a minute or two before the lift graciously consented to answer her call.

Once inside the lift Holly found herself tongue-tied. She searched her mind feverishly for some light comment to relieve the tension but it was a blank. She blessed the years of harsh training when she had learnt to disguise her feelings and appear calm and collected, however she was feeling inside, as she glanced at her reflection in the mirrored wall of the lift.

It showed an averagely tall, slim young woman with cool blue eyes and a composed face; an image she had carefully cultivated and took pleasure in. It was her wall of safety, her security, and part of her distress this morning had been because first Jeff Roberts, and then Jacques Querruel—in quite a different way from the former—had broken through the deliberately constructed barrier.

'The taxi is waiting for us.' She had been aware of his overt inspection as the lift swiftly took them downwards, but it wasn't until the doors opened in Reception that he spoke. She turned her head and looked at him then as he added, 'Your apartment is in Battersea, yes?'

'Yes.' How did he know that? Had he asked Margaret where she lived or had he checked out her personal file? The latter; she'd bet her boots on it.

'And our restaurant, Lemaires, is in Chelsea, so that is most convenient, is it not?'

She didn't know about that. The thought of Jacques Querruel sitting in the tiny bedsit which was her 'apartment' was an absolute no-go—there wasn't room to swing a cat—and the thought of him waiting outside with a taxi clocking up every minute she took to get ready wasn't an option either. As they stepped out of the smart, air-conditioned building into a pleasantly warm May evening Holly took a deep hidden breath and said steadily, 'If you would like to go on ahead to the restaurant after you've dropped me off that would be fine, Mr Querruel. I'll join you as soon as I can.'

'This is the polite English way of stating what you would prefer, I think.' The hand which was gripping her elbow felt as cool and hard through her thin cloth jacket as his voice, but as they crossed the pavement and he opened the taxi door for her he continued, 'I will send the taxi back for you, Miss Stanton. Is that acceptable? And, please, take time to refresh yourself.'

Refresh herself! As Holly slid into the taxi she had to bite back the desire to laugh out loud. She would be rushing around like a whirling dervish!

She barely noticed the taxi pull away as she began a mental list of all her clothes, desperately trying to pull an outfit worthy of Lemaires from her limited wardrobe. She'd heard of Lemaires before, of course—it was one of the very 'in' places and frequented by clientele who never had to look at the prices on the menu—but never in her wildest dreams had she imagined she'd set foot on such hallowed ground, and certainly not without at least a few hours' grace to rush out and buy something fabulous.

'...and take it from there?'

'I'm sorry?' Too late she had become aware Jacques Querruel had been speaking and she'd been miles away.

She turned to him quickly and saw he was frowning. 'I am sorry to interrupt your thoughts, Miss Stanton,' he said icily, 'but I was just outlining the way I saw the evening progressing. I suggested we could enjoy a cocktail or two as I explain my proposal, which you could think over whilst we eat, and then we will take it from there.'

Touchy, touchy. Holly got the impression it wasn't often Jacques Querruel didn't have a woman's full and undivided attention. 'Yes, of course,' she said quickly, becoming acutely aware of the close confines of the taxi for the first time as her anxiety about the clothes was put to one side for a few minutes.

He wasn't touching her—in fact there was at least six inches of space between them—but never had she been so fiercely conscious of another human being's body. She could feel the heat which had begun in the core of her spread to her throat and face as she met the amber eyes, and then, as his gaze became curiously intent, she forced herself to break the piercing hold and turned her head to look out of the window.

'It's a beautiful evening, isn't it?' she murmured quietly, managing a tone which was just offhand enough to appear genuine.

He didn't reply for a moment, but now her senses were open the subtle and delicious smell of him teased her nerves before he said softly, 'Indeed it is. Too beautiful to waste in the city streets. It is a night for breathing in the aroma of a thousand flowers as the sky slowly turns to silver. A night for watching the moonlight shimmering on a mother-of-pearl lake, and hearing the call of the wild swans as they marshal their newly fledged little ones to sleep.'

She was surprised into looking at him again, and he answered her quizzical gaze with a slow smile. 'My château.' He replied to the unspoken question very quietly. 'It is very lovely on a night like this.'

There were enough panic buttons going off in Holly's head to deafen the whole of London. 'Is it?' She smiled brightly. 'Lucky you.'

'You have been to France, Miss Stanton?'

She shook her head. She hadn't been anywhere but she wasn't about to tell him that. No doubt he was used to being in company where the merits of Switzerland or Monaco or the Caribbean were discussed with a wealth of experience.

'It is a very diverse country,' he said quietly. 'I have an apartment in Paris, close to my offices, but my real home is my château, thirty miles south of the city. It is a place of peace, a place for recharging the batteries.'

Funny, but she couldn't quite equate Jacques Querruel with peace and quiet. She kept her voice from betraying anything of what she was thinking as she said, 'You spend a lot of time there?'

'Not as much as I would like,' he said a touch ruefully. 'Part of this is my own fault, of course. I do not find it easy to delegate, Miss Stanton.'

Now, that she could believe without any trouble at all! Her face must have spoken for itself because he smiled drily. 'I think we will change the subject.'

During the rest of the twenty-minute ride to her bedsit

Holly was on tenterhooks. Not that Jacques was anything
but coolly polite and amusing, and seemingly at ease. He
sat one leg crossed casually over the other, his whole body
suggesting a relaxed composure that Holly envied with all
her heart. He didn't seem to be aware of the atmosphere
within the car, which was strange, she thought, when she
wouldn't have been surprised if the air had started to
crackle with electricity. But then she obviously registered
on him with as much force as a bowl of cold rice pudding.

The street in which her bedsit was located was not the
best in the world, and as they drew up outside the terraced
three-storey house that was identical to a hundred others
she saw Mrs Gibson's cats had been having a field-day
with the dustbins again and most of their contents were
scattered all over the minute paved front garden and the
pavement.

Holly liked Mrs Gibson, who occupied the basement
bedsit and had bright orange hair despite being eighty
years old if a day, and she didn't even mind the three cats,
who had a disconcerting habit of vomiting up their trophies from the dustbins at the most inopportune moments,
but she could have done without them today. Of course,
they had gathered *en masse* on the crumbling steps to the
front door. It was that sort of day.

The big ginger tom had just begun to lead the way in
a Mexican wave of retching as Holly leapt out of the taxi,
and she positioned herself straight in front of the car window as she said briskly, 'You really needn't send the taxi
back, Mr. Querruel. I can ring for one myself once I'm
ready.'

'I wouldn't hear of it.' He had leant forward slightly as
he spoke, his attention directed somewhere behind Holly's
left shoulder, and now he said a little bemusedly, 'There is
an elderly lady with a tea cosy on her head waving to you.'

It figured. Holly glanced behind her, waving back to Mrs Gibson before she said, 'That's Mrs Gibson. She is a friend of mine,' her tone defiant. 'I'll see you in a little while, then.'

'I will look forward to it.' The answer was polite but distracted. One of the cats had just gone for a gold medal in the realm of projectile vomiting, breaking all previous records, and Mrs Gibson was doing a kind of soft-shoe shuffle as she tried to prevent all three felines diving into the hall. Jacques looked fascinated.

As the taxi drew away Holly turned round, her tone resigned as she said, 'I'll get a bucket of water and some disinfectant and clear all this up, Mrs Gibson.'

'Would you, Holly? There's a dear. Mr Bateman, the silly old fool, has gone and put kippers in the dustbins again. I told him Tigger would have the lids off before you could blink, but would he listen? The man's an idiot.'

'Mrs Gibson, why are you wearing a tea cosy on your head?' Holly asked matter-of-factly.

'Am I, dear? Well, there's a thing!' Mrs Gibson blinked at her as she removed the offending article from her sparse bright hair and then giggled like a schoolgirl. 'I've been wondering where this was for a few days. I must have put it on the coat stand instead of my woolly hat when I washed them both. I wonder what I've done with the hat, because it isn't on the teapot.'

'Don't worry about it,' Holly said, smiling into the pert little face which was as wrinkled and lined as a pink prune. 'It'll turn up.'

By the time Holly had cleared up after the cats and weighed down the dustbins with two bricks apiece, kept specially for the purpose but rarely used by anyone but herself, she'd lost ten minutes of valuable time.

She dashed up to her bedsit on the first floor, stripping off her clothes and flinging on her robe before hurtling along to the bathroom at the end of her landing. A quick two-minute shower in cold water—the water heater was playing up again—ensured a bracing if teeth-chattering pick-me-up, and then she was back to the bedsit, pulling off her shower cap and standing in front of her wardrobe as she surveyed her sum total of clothes.

She had one or two really nice things, she thought despairingly, but were they suitable for somewhere like Lemaires? She doubted it, but nevertheless the black and blue ruched and printed bandeau dress and vertiginous high heels she had bought to celebrate securing the job at Querruel International would have to do. If nothing else the shoes would give her an extra few inches, which wouldn't go amiss considering Jacques Querruel had seemed to tower over her in the lift, and her black wrap— the bargain of the year twelve months before, when she'd spied the beautiful Versace wrap in a charity shop for a fraction of its original price—would dress up the whole outfit.

She peeped out of the window before she went to work with her make-up and the taxi was already back and waiting. No time to put her hair up, then. She contented herself with eyeshadow and mascara, along with a careful application of her lipstick pencil, finishing her toilette with a dab of perfume on her wrists. Silver studs in her ears and a silver bangle on one wrist and she was ready. She stood in front of the mirror, breathing deeply in and out for a moment or two. She had never felt so scared in all her life.

'Look at it this way,' she said to the wide-eyed, dark-haired girl staring back at her from out of the mirror. 'You have got nothing to lose and everything to gain from hearing what he has to say. You'd already decided you wouldn't be able to stay at Querruel International, not working for Margaret anyway. He might, he just *might* make you an offer you can't refuse.'

No, she hadn't phrased that quite right, Holly thought agitatedly as the mental image of a tall, dark and extremely handsome Frenchman sent the juices flowing. What she'd meant was, she might find she didn't have to start the dismal rounds of searching out the right kind of job again.

She would hear him out, weigh up the pros and cons of what he said and then make an informed decision. Simple. No big deal, not really, not unless she made it one. OK, so he was taking her to dinner, but he'd been pretty nonchalant about it. He clearly hadn't been over-bothered one way or the other. And that was fine. Great. Perfect. The last thing she needed was for him to get any sort of ideas.

She gathered up her small black purse and the wrap, and squared her slim shoulders as though she was going into battle instead of to dinner. But that was what it felt like…

Jacques saw her the moment she walked through the doors of Lemaires; he had been watching the entrance intently ever since he had sat down at the secluded little table for two. He rose immediately and raised his hand, and as the waiter guided her over to him he said quietly, 'Thank you, Claude. And perhaps you would bring one of your delicious champagne cocktails for Miss Stanton?'

Once she was seated, Holly said a little breathlessly, 'I hope I haven't kept you waiting too long, Mr Querruel.'

'Not at all,' Jacques said pleasantly. He had settled back in his seat once she was comfortable, his eyes unreadable and his big body relaxed.

Holly envied him. She felt as taut as piano wire. Whether her tenseness communicated itself to him she didn't know, but he took the wind out of her sails completely in the next moment when he leant forward and said quietly, 'In view of the surroundings I think we could be less formal, don't you? Loosen up a little—is that the phrase? My name is Jacques and yours is Holly, I understand? An unusual name, even for someone born at the end of December.'

So he *had* looked up her file. Holly felt horribly flustered even as she told herself she'd known it all along. Jacques Querruel was the type of man who would want every fact at his fingertips before he talked about a job offer. But there were a hundred and one things one could never learn from the anonymous black print of a personnel file.

And this was borne out when Jacques continued, 'Your mother's choice of name or your father's?'

'Neither.' She purposely didn't elaborate, hoping he would take the hint and accept a change of subject when she continued, 'It's very kind of you to buy me dinner, Mr Querruel, but it really wasn't necessary.'

The amber eyes moved over her face very slowly before he said, 'Yes, it was. And the name's Jacques.' His gaze intensified, the thick black lashes adding to the piercing quality. 'And if it was not your parents who gave you your name, then who did?' he persisted softly.

'The sister in charge of the maternity unit where I was taken after being abandoned.' She didn't try to soften the statement. '"The Holly and the Ivy" was playing on the radio when they brought me in.'

He didn't come back with any of the comments she might have expected and had experienced in the past on the rare occasions the circumstances of her birth had become known, but then she should have known he wouldn't. He was not a flock animal. He merely expelled a silent breath before saying, 'Tough start. Very tough.'

She nodded tightly. 'Yes, it was.'

'Did they find the woman who had given birth to you?'

She was glad he hadn't called Angela Stanton her mother, because for a long time now she had understood the biological ability to produce did not make a mother. She nodded again. 'At the point she gave birth to me she'd already got three children, all by different fathers; she didn't want a fourth,' she said evenly. 'After she was traced she visited me once or twice, I understand, but that's all. I contacted her when I was twenty-one and we met briefly; she was happy to tell me anything I wanted to know. My father was a married man she'd had a short affair with. She didn't tell me his name and I didn't ask. All her other children were put in care at some point and are in various parts of the country. There were two more after me.'

Her mouth was unyielding and set in a controlled line. Ridiculously he wanted to kiss the warm fullness back. The strength of his feeling shocked him and his mouth was dry when he said, 'I am truly sorry, Holly.'

She shrugged, and he realised the gesture went hand in hand with the closed expression on her face. Both were too old for a young woman of twenty-five. 'It happens,' she said dismissively. 'And lots of people suffer worse every day.'

The waiter arrived with two long fluted glasses filled to the brim with sparkling, effervescent liquid, and Jacques watched her face change as she looked up at the balding, middle-aged man, smiling her thanks. She hadn't liked talking about herself. She hadn't liked it at all. And she didn't like him. He felt his pulse quicken and didn't know if the feeling coursing through him was desire, pique, excitement or curiosity, or maybe a mixture of them all.

He took control of himself and the situation, raising his glass and touching hers in a toast as he said lightly, 'To an excellent meal and a good bottle of wine when it comes.'

Holly laughed; she couldn't help it. 'That's a little self-indulgent, isn't it?' she commented just as lightly.

'Perhaps.' He smiled at her, a social, easy smile. 'But it's to your benefit too.'

'True.' She considered, her head slightly tilted to one side. 'All right, then. To the meal and the wine.'

The cocktail was delicious but she could feel the bubbles going straight to her head, and too late Holly told herself she should have eaten something earlier. She hadn't had a bite since lunch and even then she had only nibbled at a sandwich, the events of the morning ruining her appetite. She took a firm hold on herself, putting the glass down and fixing the dark, handsome face opposite with what she hoped was an efficient, matter-of-fact expression as she said, 'You mentioned a job proposition?' She would have liked to add 'Mr Querruel' but he had insisted she call him Jacques earlier, and she couldn't, she just *couldn't* bring herself to do that. Consequently the question just trailed to a finish.

'Later. You need to unwind.'

Did she? She didn't think she did. In fact she thought it imperative she didn't 'unwind', as he put it. She needed to have all her wits about her tonight. But he was the big boss and she couldn't very well argue. She wriggled her bottom nervously; she was out of her depth here. Margaret was right; she shouldn't have accepted this ridiculous invitation to dinner.

'And stop looking at me as though you are little Red Riding Hood and I am the big bad wolf,' Jacques said softly, his accent lending a resonance to the words that sent a little shiver right down her spine. 'Tell me about Mrs Gibson instead, and your apartment. Are any of your other neighbours so colourful?'

'It's not an apartment, it's a bedsit,' said Holly after a fortifying sip of champagne. 'There's a big difference there, you know. And Mrs Gibson is just a dear old lady who's marvellous for her age and a trifle eccentric. Perhaps more than a trifle.'

She slipped the wrap from her shoulders as she spoke and saw his eyes follow the movement, their light resting on the creamy skin before moving downwards to where the soft swell of her breasts were just visible above the bodice of the dress. And then he raised his eyes back to her hot face, not even trying to pretend he wasn't looking as he said, 'You look very beautiful, Holly.'

Perhaps it was his French accent, or the incredible lush surroundings and glittering occupants of the restaurant, or just the fact she was trying to hide how overwhelmed she felt, but Holly felt a nervous giggle escape before she could bite it back. This was so utterly, *completely* silver-screen material!

'I have amused you?' It was frosty and his expression had changed to one of chilled hauteur.

Oh, help. Holly took a deep breath. 'Of course not.'

'But something has.'

She stared at him across the small table covered in thick cream linen, a single white rose in a silver vase perfuming the air, and for no reason at all that she could name Holly suddenly rebelled against his autocracy. 'It's all this,' she said before she had a chance to think too hard about what she was going to say. 'It's not real life, is it? Of course, it's very nice...' Her voice trailed away.

'Oh, thank you.' His voice dripped with sarcasm.

'No, really, it *is* very lovely as a treat.' She was making this worse, she realised helplessly. Much worse. And when all was said and done he *had* brought her out to this fabulous restaurant where everything was so gorgeous and special. It was just that everyone seemed to take themselves so seriously, she supposed. And she'd been fighting taking herself seriously—or anyone else for that matter—all her life. She didn't like this last thought and so she filed it away to look at again later.

Silence had fallen. Jacques was sitting with his glass held loosely between his fingers as it rested on the table, his eyes on her flushed face.

Holly nerved herself to meet the amber gaze, which she was sure would be as coldly sarcastic as his voice, but as their eyes caught and held she felt the weird electrical current she'd sensed in the taxi. Her heartbeat went haywire, and suddenly the whole world was narrowed down to one small table and two pairs of eyes.

'So you are not a woman who expects to be wined and dined and spoilt?' he asked very, very softly. 'In spite of being so beautiful. What is the matter with your English men, *ma chérie*?'

Holly's eyes widened and for a full ten seconds she found herself speechless. He was flirting with her— Jacques Querruel? *Jacques Querruel.* And nothing in her past had prepared her for how to handle this. It had always been one of her rigid rules to keep her distance—literally—from men. To avoid their touch, their invasion into her air space. Which was why Jeff Roberts had annoyed her so much. She loathed men like him who thought they had some preordained right to make advances to any female they liked, to touch and maul and manhandle. And so it had been easier to keep the whole pack of them at arm's length; that way no one had any excuse for getting the wrong idea.

She grabbed her glass and tossed back the last of the champagne cocktail. Its fortifying effects enabled her to say, fairly evenly, 'Nothing is the matter with English men as far as I know,' before following up with a bright, artificial smile.

'But you do not have a boyfriend, a partner?'

'The same could be said for thousands of women, surely?'

She pushed back her sleek veil of hair as she spoke and he saw her eyes were violet with defiance and something else he didn't recognise. He had touched a nerve here. Careful not to appear anything but relaxed and casual, Jacques said easily, 'Maybe, but not often ones with eyes the colour of your English cornflowers and hair of warm, silky chocolate. When was your last love affair, Holly?'

She moved back in her seat, an instinctive but very revealing gesture. He waited, without saying a word.

The waiter returned with two terrifyingly chic and elegant menus, placing them in their hands with almost reverent decorum before taking an order from Jacques for two more cocktails. Holly wanted to protest but she didn't. Somehow she felt she would need the boost the alcohol gave her to survive this evening intact.

The waiter having glided off to get the drinks, Jacques peered at her over the top of his open menu. 'The Chinese black bean and green pepper chicken is good to start with,' he suggested smoothly, pretending not to notice as her eyes ran anxiously over the pages, which were all in

French. Double Dutch to Holly. 'And it complements the coriander salmon with mango perfectly. Trust me?'

She met his gaze. Trusting Jacques Querruel was not an option! 'That sounds very nice,' she said primly.

'Oh, it is nice,' he assured her gravely as the waiter returned with the cocktails. After he had given their order for the food and wine and they were alone again, Jacques relaxed back in his seat once more. 'So, the last boyfriend,' he said silkily. 'The love of your life or just another young hopeful?'

The question hammered at her aplomb and there was a moment of silence so charged she knew he'd sensed it. She had lowered her eyes and she took a long, hidden breath before staring straight at him. 'There hasn't been much time for boyfriends,' she said coolly.

His pulse quickened. What the hell did that mean? 'No?'

'No.'

He was damned if he was going to leave it at that. 'Why not, Holly?' he asked quietly.

She had been sipping at her cocktail and now plonked her glass down with an air of Oh, for goodness' sake! Which Jacques ignored.

He wasn't going to leave this alone until she'd spelt it out for him, was he? Holly thought tensely. She wished she could just walk out of here and go home, but that would be way, way over the top. He hadn't insulted her or been difficult in any way; most people would class this as perfectly acceptable social intercourse.

Bright patches of colour staining the creamy skin of her cheeks, Holly said, 'I stayed on at school until eighteen to finish my A levels and then left to get a job and somewhere to live. I worked for two years so I could put myself through university without entering into a whole load of debt with loans and such. I worked long hours; there was no time for a social life.'

'Why did you leave home as well as school?'

'I didn't have a home!' It was a snap, and Holly warned herself to take control of her voice before she said more calmly, 'What I mean is I lived in a foster home and I didn't get on with the rest of the family particularly well. It was better for everyone I left and, besides, I was too old to continue with them. I finished university when I was twenty-three and have had one other job besides my present one. I made up my mind to be a career girl and concentrate on my work rather than a love life.'

He didn't buy this. He did not buy this at all. 'Very sensible,' he said understandingly. 'But you enjoyed yourself at university no doubt?'

She ignored the meaning behind the words. 'I had a great time,' she agreed stiffly.

Jacques wanted to push some more but now was not the time. 'Everyone does,' he remarked drily. 'Raging hormones and hundreds of young people let loose for the first time in their lives makes for some interesting diary reading.' And then he completely backtracked on his earlier decision as he said, 'Did you keep a diary, Holly?' making sure his voice suggested amusement and nothing of the burning curiosity he was feeling.

He was watching her closely, seriously, despite the smile on his lips, and Holly had the feeling they were fencing like two duellists, one of which was hopelessly ill-equipped. She made an enormous effort and said lightly, 'I prefer reading to writing.'

'Yes?' His voice was smoky. 'But this is such a solitary pursuit, is it not? Two cannot play at this.' He shifted in his seat, shrugging off his suit jacket just as the waiter appeared with their first course. Once the food was in front of them Jacques leant forward slightly, forcing her to acknowledge her own awareness of him as he said, his hand gesturing at his tie, 'Do you mind? I always feel as if these things are strangling me.'

'No, not at all,' she gulped hastily, still reeling from the way her senses had tingled at his nearness. He pulled the tie loose, undoing the first couple of buttons of his shirt, and she could see the beginnings of the dark body hair which must cover his chest. She finished the champagne cocktail and reached for the glass of wine the waiter had poured after serving their first course. And then she put it down again. She had to eat something, she warned herself feverishly. She was going to be tipsy at this rate and that would never do.

It wasn't hard to continue eating once she had tasted the chicken, in spite of her jangling nerves. The food was absolutely delicious, and the TV dinner she had been going to pull out of the freezer compartment of her little fridge couldn't begin to compete.

It helped that with the arrival of the food Jacques had metamorphosed into Mr Congeniality, his conversation humorous and diverting and his manner amiable.

After the main course, which was even more delicious than the one before, the waiter brought the dessert menus. Jacques quietly talked her through the delectable list in such a way she didn't feel in the least embarrassed at her lack of knowledge.

'Chocolate terrine ribboned in caramel sounds lovely,' Holly said wistfully, 'but the orange and strawberry granita with liqueur muscat chantilly sounds pretty good too.'

'We'll have one of each and share.'

She stared at him, frankly horrified, her stomach clenching. Ridiculously, it seemed far too intimate to share puddings. 'No, it's all right,' Holly said hastily. 'I'll choose one.'

'No need.' He said it as casually as if he hadn't noticed the look on her face, and as the ever-attentive waiter materialised at their sides like a genie out of a bottle Holly realised it was a *fait accompli*. As most things seemed to be around Jacques Querruel.

It was in that moment she understood the last hour or so had lulled her into a state of false security. She still didn't have a clue what this evening was all about, or what the job offer comprised, and she'd been with him for—she surreptitiously glanced at her wrist-watch—over two hours. She had to get things back to a more…official footing. She took a sip of wine, wiped her mouth carefully with her napkin and opened her mouth to speak. She was a moment too late.

'So, Holly.' The air of charming companion had fallen away from him like a cloak; Jacques was suddenly very much the millionaire tycoon. 'To business. You took your degree in textiles, yes? What are you doing sitting behind a desk typing reports?'

Holly stiffened, recognising all over again that he was dangerous. She stared at him for a moment before she said, 'There were no openings in the areas I was interested in, besides which I also took business studies. I thought it would be good to get an all-round knowledge of Querruel International and—'

'I need a textile technologist responsive to design, and enthusiasm is more important to me than experience,' Jacques stated impatiently, cutting into her words with all the ruthlessness she'd sensed in him. 'You would work hand in hand with my designers and the rest of the team to produce high-quality, sophisticated products that will sell in the UK and overseas. Querruel International is efficient and competitive but we need more flexibility, more innovation. Do you understand what I am saying?'

She nodded, breathless.

'I would offer a three-month contract to begin with, to see how you fit into the team. Most of them have been with me since I started and it's imperative to maintain a good working relationship,' Jacques went on evenly. 'They are all well-qualified people of the right calibre and all fiercely loyal to Querruel International. I will accept nothing less. Remuneration is accordingly high.' He mentioned a starting salary that made Holly grateful she was sitting down. It was four times more than she was presently earning. 'For this I demand working round the clock when it is necessary, which is not often,' he added with the ghost of a smile. 'You will not be expected to be perfect but you will be expected to give Querruel International one hundred per cent commitment.'

Holly couldn't believe her ears. This was the once-in-a-lifetime chance, the crock of gold at the end of the rainbow. She could work for years and years and years and not be given an opportunity like this one again.

'So, Holly, are you interested in hearing more?' he asked quietly, his eyes intent on her flushed, excited face. 'What are you thinking?'

'Mainly how soon can I start?' she answered breathlessly.

'As soon as you can organise a passport and your affairs in England.'

Holly floundered. He wasn't saying…

'The job would require you moving to Paris,' Jacques stated expressionlessly, seeing the sudden dawning of understanding in her face. 'I thought you understood this?'

No. She hadn't understood that at all.

CHAPTER THREE

WHEN Holly awoke the next morning it was to the sound of pouring rain outside her window, and the knowledge that she had tossed and turned half the night.

The grey sky and greasy streets were as different from the previous lovely, warm day as could be, and they reflected rather aptly how twenty-four hours could bring about mind-boggling change, she thought, standing in the crush of a rush-hour underground train.

Yesterday she had been content. She had had the security of a good job with long-term prospects and the bolt-hole of her little home. OK, the bedsit might not be everyone's idea of Utopia, but in the months she had been living there since leaving university she had made it her own. For the first time in her life she'd been able to relax knowing *she* decided who walked through the door. Her autonomy had been hard-won and precious.

Holly turned her head, staring at her murky reflection in the dirty train window. Now she was in utter confusion. On the one hand she faced the uncertainty and trauma of trying to secure another job with the same scope for bettering herself in the future the present one had promised, and on the other...

She moved carefully—sandwiched as she was between an enormous lady with a very large briefcase and a young teenager with pink hair and black lipstick—and brushed her hair away from her face.

On the other hand there was the enormity of a move to Paris and everything—and everyone—that entailed. And the everyone narrowed down to one very strong and charismatic Frenchman if she was being truthful.

Jacques Querruel had been more than fair last night, though; she had to admit that. He had guaranteed to provide an excellent reference should she decide to stay in England and look for another position here, whilst assuring her there was no need for her to leave her current job at Querruel International unless she wished to do so. He would make sure she was not—he'd hesitated there for a moment, she remembered—pressurised for her decision to make a complaint against Jeff Roberts. Which sounded fine in theory.

The train pulled in to a station and the girl with candy-floss hair and black lips got off. Everyone shuffled about a bit as new passengers boarded, and they were off again, even more tightly packed than before. She hated this, the Underground. At least in the rush hour. The press of bodies and the warmth and the smells. Like today. Damp, fusty clothes and the odour of rain on hair that had absorbed the smell of cooking the night before. As with the lady next to her with the briefcase.

Holly brought her mind back resolutely to the problem in hand. Jacques Querruel had also said that, until the three-month trial period was over and all parties concerned had declared themselves happy with the status quo, he would arrange for payment for her bedsit to continue as normal, with no deduction from her salary. Which was amazingly generous and reasonable and… She sighed irritably. If she told any of her friends about this they would think she was crazy not to give the job in Paris a go. And she would, she would like a shot, except for *him*.

She sighed again, and then, as she caught the eye of the lady with the briefcase, realised the woman had misinterpreted her huffing and puffing as a complaint against the current sardines-in-a-tin situation. Holly smiled weakly into the stony face and exited smartly at the next station, which thankfully was her own.

The offices of Querruel International were just a short two-minute walk from the subway, but it was time enough for Holly's stomach to tie itself into knots.

He hadn't made a move on her last night—not that she'd expected the illustrious head of Querruel International to do that with a mere minion anyway—and had been friendly and amusing, so why was she so—she refused to accept the word 'frightened' in her mind and substituted—nervous about the possibility of working in close proximity to this man? She was just an employee to him, one of hundreds, and but for the fact he had overheard her confrontation with Jeff yesterday he wouldn't know her from Adam.

OK, so he was clearly a sensual man, dynamic, dangerous, a man to be avoided where possible, but she avoided anything of a personal nature with all men.

Perhaps it was because he made her feel edgy and jittery around him? Or because, unlike with other men, she couldn't weigh Jacques Querruel up and give him a label in her mind? Even the creeps like Jeff Roberts were easy to identify, and once that had been accomplished they became no threat where it mattered—in her head.

She came to the steps of Querruel International and stood on the pavement for a moment, despite the pouring rain. She didn't want to see him again, she really didn't, so why were there little *frissons* of something she couldn't put a name to shivering down her spine?

Once inside the building she walked over to the lift and pressed the button, and after the doors had slid open and then shut again she found she was alone in the mirrored box. She turned and inspected herself, tidying her hair and checking her mascara hadn't smudged, and as she stared at her reflection something in her eyes brought her heart thudding into her throat.

No. The answer to the Paris job had to be no. She knew it did. He was too disturbing, too threatening to be around. The aggressive sexuality that was part of his persona might send some women weak at the knees but she didn't like it. She became aware her hands were shaking slightly and made a sound of quiet self-disgust low in her throat. What on earth was the matter with her? This man wasn't omnipotent, for goodness' sake, although he'd just love it if he knew she'd got herself into a bit of a state over him!

As the lift glided to a halt and the doors began to open Holly did what she had been doing all her life. She straightened her drooping shoulders, lifted her chin and narrowed her eyes, clothing herself with an invisible armour of cool detachment. Jacques Querruel had not, and would not, get under her skin. She wouldn't let him.

Last night had admittedly been a little…overwhelming, but she was back on turf she understood now and it was broad daylight. She would thank him politely for the opportunity to work in Paris when she saw him today, decline gracefully and that would be that. And she *would* leave Querruel International as soon as she could, even if she had to take a drop in salary. In fact she could temp for a time; she'd temped through all the university holidays and the agency she had used then would be glad to have her back. She'd go and see them this weekend, or even tonight.

She stepped out of the lift determinedly, turned a smart left and found herself in Jacques Querruel's arms, the file he had been holding spreading its papers all over the floor as he dropped it in an endeavour to steady them both.

Too late Holly realised she had been miles away in a

world of her own instead of concentrating on what was in front of her nose. Strong arms were holding her firmly, and as she looked up into clear amber eyes she was alarmingly conscious of a whiff of subtle lemony aftershave.

'Good morning.' It was an amused, throaty murmur and brought even more hot colour flooding into her cheeks, which were already a bright shade of pink.

'Oh, I'm sorry, Mr Querruel.' But for his quick thinking she would have ended up in an ungainly heap on the floor with the force of their impact and the high heels she was wearing. She had power-dressed that morning: her new salmon suit with its pencil-slim skirt ending just above her knees and court shoes that were just high enough to make her ankles fragile.

Jacques was wearing the suit of the night before but with a different shirt and tie in pale charcoal. He looked devastating. Her brain made no apology for the word. Even following up with, utterly drop-dead gorgeous.

'I thought we decided last night it was ''Jacques''?'

He was still holding her and she was so mesmerised that she made no move to free herself. 'But that was away from the office,' Holly said weakly.

'And this is *in* the office and I still wish you to call me by my first name, *mademoiselle*.'

He smiled, and panic warred with enchantment. But only for a moment. Panic won. Holly pulled away, breaking the contact between them and taking hold of her fluttering heart as she did so. 'I don't think that is wise,' she said quickly. 'People might get the wrong idea.'

'Why?' He knelt down to pick up the papers as he spoke and her eyes were drawn as if by a magnet to muscled, lean thighs. 'And what the hell is it to do with anyone else anyway? I am the boss, am I not? I can do whatever I want.'

It was so charmingly boyish she was fascinated. She stared at him for a full ten seconds before she remembered to speak. 'That's not really the point, is it?' she said, but not as firmly as she would have liked.

'Oh, but it is exactly the point.' He stood up again, and any impression of boyishness was gone as she stared up into the hard masculine face that was a good six inches above hers despite the heels. 'I do not allow anyone to dictate to me, Holly. I never have done. My father always used to say that I would either be locked away in prison by the time I was twenty-one or on the way to making my first million. Fortunately it was the latter.'

He grinned, and she smiled weakly back. The wearing of her suit, her careful make-up and discreet dab of perfume that morning had been in the form of a silent declaration that she was perfectly in control of her feelings and her life, she realised now. A statement that nothing had changed in the last twenty-four hours. She had been kidding herself.

'I'm sure your father is relieved about that,' she managed fairly normally.

'I think this is so,' he agreed softly, 'and for my mother too. I have two younger sisters who are very beautiful and she worries about them constantly as they are both still—how do you say—playing the field, yes? So it is a relief that one of her ducklings is a pillar of the establishment.'

Pillar of the establishment? Jacques Querruel? Never! Holly smiled politely before she said, 'I had better let Margaret know I've arrived.'

'Of course.' The amber eyes held hers for a second, and then he nodded before moving swiftly down the corridor towards the managing director's secretary's domain.

Holly found herself staring after him. His voice worried her—it was so deep and smoky, and the accent gave it a kick of pure sensuality. His manner worried her—it was one of autocratic authority, however reasonable he gave the impression of being. *He* worried her—there was a sort of dark power about him that made it seem utterly feasible that he had risen from obscurity to dizzy heights in a decade. Vitality and strength radiated from him and it gave her the crazy desire to run and keep running.

Fanciful! She gave a half-smile and shook her head at her whimsical thoughts. And it wasn't like her. She was the last person in the world to indulge in capricious flights of fancy.

She would simply tell him later in the day before he left for France that she had considered his kind offer but it was no, thanks. Simple.

'So?' Margaret's head shot up as Holly entered the office. 'How did you get on last night?'

'Let me get my coat off,' Holly said, laughing a little at the very un-Margaret-like urgency. If anyone in the world was calm and unflappable it was Mr. Roberts's capable and organised secretary.

'Mr Querruel's left some papers for your attention on your desk,' Margaret volunteered as Holly walked across the room. It was clear the other woman was burning with curiosity. 'Said they related to your discussions last night?'

'He offered me a job on his team in France.' Holly walked through and slipped off her jacket, hanging it on the back of her chair as Margaret appeared in the doorway to the cubby-hole. 'I said I'd think about it. Textile technologist. It's what I've always hoped to get involved in eventually, but…'

'There's a but? Holly, are you mad?' Margaret breathed quietly, coming right up to the desk where Holly was now sitting and bending forward as she whispered, 'Accept quickly before he changes his mind or something. I know people who would give their eye-teeth to be part of his élite team in France. I'm not kidding. Why are you even thinking about it for more than one second?'

Holly stared into the plump, homely face. 'Margaret, you were the one who warned me off him yesterday,' she reminded her soberly.

'That was when I thought he was…well, you know,' Margaret returned quickly. 'But this is different. If he's offered you a job it means he's not interested in anything more; he's renowned for never mixing business and pleasure.'

Holly nodded. That was good news, wasn't it? Of course it was. So why the flat feeling in the pit of her stomach?

They heard the buzzer on Margaret's desk sound, long and hard, and Margaret grimaced as she murmured, 'Mr Roberts is in a filthy fit; I'd better go. And keep your head down whilst he's about. He's out all afternoon so we can relax a bit then.'

Great. This wet Tuesday morning was just getting better and better.

Once Holly was alone she took a deep breath as she looked at the large manila envelope lying on her desk. It was bulging and sealed, with her name written across it in a bold black script she just knew was Jacques's handwriting. Well, she could look at what it contained, couldn't she? That didn't mean she was going to change her mind.

Fifteen minutes later her mind was changed. The work sounded exciting and interesting, the salary was phenomenal with added bonuses Jacques hadn't mentioned last night, and the package included Querruel International finding a place for her to rent until the three-month trial period was over, at which point they were prepared to pay full relocation expenses. She had nothing to lose and everything to gain. And he wasn't interested in her. Margaret had said so. Not that she had imagined for one minute he was, of course.

Jacques had said the night before that he was leaving England about mid-afternoon, so when—at just gone eleven—he appeared in the doorway of her room dressed for the road and his Harley-Davidson, Holly stared at him in surprise.

'Change of plan.' He answered the unspoken question abruptly. 'I need to leave early.'

'Oh.' She nodded, the colour rushing into her face. 'I...I've looked at all the data you left this morning and I would like to accept your offer, Mr Querruel.'

'Good.' His eyes narrowed, the amber light brilliant against his black lashes. 'But all my immediate team in Paris are on Christian-name terms, OK? Does this make ''Jacques'' any safer?'

There was sufficient innuendo for Holly to feel she had been put in her place by an expert. 'I don't know what you mean,' she lied quickly.

'No?' He alarmed her by walking into the room, pushing aside some papers as he perched easily on her desk, his eyes skimming over her face. 'This is not true, I think. You like the idea of the job but you do not like the idea of working too closely with me. Or is it any man, I wonder?' The tone was mocking. 'No, I think it is me, *n'est-ce pas*?'

'That's ridiculous,' Holly said stiffly.

'Maybe.' He smiled, one hand reaching out and tilting her face up to meet the full scrutiny of the cool eyes. 'Maybe not. It does not matter. I need a new textile technologist. You seem to fit the bill. I will advise my secretary, Chantal, to make all the necessary arrangements; please do not concern yourself with anything but being ready to leave in two weeks' time. She will contact you tomorrow. *Au revoir*, Holly.'

'But where will I live in France? And what about the hearing concerning Mr Roberts?' Everything was happening much too fast.

'Chantal will take care of these things.' He let go of her, standing to his feet. His face was remote now, cold, and she had the feeling he had already left the building and was mentally in Paris, dealing with whatever the problem was. For a second she had the absurd urge to do something to get his attention, but she curbed it instantly.

Instead she said calmly and politely, 'Goodbye, then. I hope you have a pleasant journey.'

'Oh, I shall, Holly.' He glanced towards her tiny window. 'See, the sun is already making an appearance.'

So even the weather was under his control!

Holly wasn't aware her thoughts had shown on her face but when Jacques gave a small laugh, low in his throat, she said quickly, 'What's the matter?'

'Nothing,' he said softly. 'Not a thing. I shall not return to England before you join us in Paris, but if you wish to speak to me at any time before this you can ring the office. If I am not there my secretary will advise you where I am. If you find it is necessary to speak to me out of working hours my home numbers are on this card. The top one is my apartment in Paris, but I am rarely there unless there is some emergency or other which keeps me in the office most of the time. The other is my château. Monique will probably answer the call. She is my housekeeper, you understand?'

Understand? She didn't understand a thing where this man was concerned. She had never felt so disturbed in her life. Holly smiled coolly. 'I'm sure it won't be necessary to bother you, Mr...'

The amber eyes dared her to continue.

'Jacques,' she substituted stiffly.

He nodded. 'I too am sure. You will make certain of this, I think.'

There was a definite edge to the smooth voice, like silk draped over finely honed steel, but before Holly could respond in any way he walked over to the door. He turned in the doorway and his tone was quite different when he said, 'It is the right decision to spread your wings, Holly. Be assured of this. In Paris you will find out who the real Holly is.'

She stared at him in amazement. 'I know who I am,' she said at last. 'I told you, I found out all the details of my birth.'

'I was not thinking of your beginnings,' he said softly. Did she realise how beautiful she was? It was strange but he rather thought not, and that was unusual. Certainly among the women he knew. But then, maybe he knew the wrong sort of women? He didn't like this thought any more than the fact that he had found himself unable to sleep the night before. Images of her had raced through his head and kept him awake until dawn, and this was not acceptable. He had not experienced this before. Jacques collected his thoughts, filed them away in a box in his head and slammed the lid down hard.

'*Au revoir,*' he said again, giving her a curt nod, and then he turned and walked away. Holly heard the door to Margaret's office open and close and then silence.

She sat for some moments more, staring at the space where he had been, her head whirling. And then she stood up and walked over to the small, narrow window. She had always considered the view uninspiring, considering it consisted of the entrance and exit to the company car park situated in the bowels of the building, but now she found her heart thudding.

She stood quietly peering out, willing Margaret to remain ensconced in Michael Roberts's office, where she had been for the past half an hour, and after a few minutes her patience was rewarded. The motorbike was a beauty, a magnificent black and silver monster which paused briefly before roaring off, but it was the black figure controlling the beautiful colossus which drew her gaze. Jacques was crouched over the beast, helmet in place, but she could almost see the narrowed amber eyes intent on the road ahead, the single-minded concentration pulling his mouth into a stern line and tensing the muscles of the big masculine body.

She watched the bike and rider until they disappeared round a corner in a blaze of silver and black, and then gave a deep, shuddering sigh. She'd been mad to accept the job. She had known it but she'd still done it. Which meant, whatever happened, she'd walked into this with her eyes wide open. Not exactly a comforting thought…

Reseated at her desk, Holly made no attempt to continue with the pile of work awaiting her attention. He had accused her of wanting the job but disliking the idea of working with him, and he had been right in a way. She worried at her bottom lip with small white teeth. Yes, he had been right. He was too male, too vigorous, too strong. She had nothing against dynamic, energetic men in the workplace, she had worked with a few in her previous job, but not one of them had been remotely like Jacques Querruel. There was something about him which panicked her and she didn't understand it.

She shut her eyes tightly, the memories which she always kept buried surfacing in spite of herself. Suddenly she was eight years old again, upset and unhappy at being moved from the foster parents who had cared for her since she was a few months old.

She had loved Kate and Angus West dearly, and had looked on their other two foster children, who were younger than her, and their two natural children, who were much older, as her brothers and sisters. But within weeks of Angus being diagnosed with a rare form of bone cancer his wife had had a severe stroke, brought about by shock and stress, according to the doctors, and the little family Holly had looked upon as hers had been fragmented.

David and Cassie Kirby had been very different from the middle-aged and homely Kate and Angus, and everyone—social workers, teachers and so on—had assumed she was just finding the change of home and lifestyle strange and unsettling. David and Cassie had lived in a massive six-bedroomed house with four bathrooms and a swimming pool; Holly had her own bedroom, a wardrobe full of new clothes, riding lessons—she would adapt and love it. Of course she would. What child wouldn't? And the other two children who lived with David and Cassie adored their foster parents.

Holly had heard this accolade repeated over and over again in the next six months, but then, just before her ninth birthday, she'd understood why she felt uneasy and frightened around the charismatic, handsome and wealthy David. Understood why she didn't like his kisses and hugs, his encouragement for her to sit on his knee, to be his 'little princess'.

She hadn't understood what he was trying to do when he'd come to her bedroom that night. He had come before, ostensibly to check her homework or have what he called his 'daddy talks', but this time he hadn't stopped at hugging her close and touching her in the scary way, and kissing her with his mouth wide open. But she hadn't been like his other foster children, probably because they had been with David and Cassie since they were babies and they were completely under his control.

She had resisted what he'd wanted her to do to him, and he to her, refusing to be swayed by first his pleas and then his threats, and even though his superior strength had overcome her struggles in the end she had still managed to thwart his intention, which was nothing short of rape.

He had locked her in her room after he left, and when she had cried and banged on the door and Cassie had come she'd heard him telling his wife some story about her cheeking him.

She had tried to tell Cassie what had happened the next morning, before she'd left for school, but David's wife had been furious with her for 'telling such wicked, wicked lies', whisking her upstairs and locking her in her bedroom again. And then she had learnt how powerful David was. He had forced the other two children—a boy and a girl—to say Holly had regularly attacked them, that she had destroyed their homework, wrecked their toys and so on. That she was unruly and out of hand. She had stolen small trinkets from the house and probably from local shops, he had stated to the social worker he'd called in. She was running amok and although they had tried everything, bending over backwards to keep her, they sadly had to admit defeat. For the sake of the other children. And neither Cassie or the other children had lifted a finger to help her.

She had been labelled a problem and had been too scared to continue to press her accusations, too hurt and confused. The next home had been a disaster from day one. A sense of bitter, impotent injustice compounded by a paralysing fear at any overture of friendship by a member of the opposite sex—especially one in authority over her—had set the tone for the next few years. Years of being moved from one place to another; of always being the odd one out; of being lonely and alone.

Looking back from an adult viewpoint, she now saw that many of the grown-ups she had come into contact with through that time had tried to help her, but her treatment at the hands of David and Cassie Kirby had made her hostile and suspicious. But she had survived...

Holly opened her eyes, breathing deeply to control her racing heartbeat. She had made a life for herself on her own terms and without asking help from anyone, and she had collected a few friends along the way. Of course, they were mostly female, apart from dear old Mr Bateman at the top of the house, who was seventy-five years old and pining from unrequited love for Mrs Gibson, and James Holden, one of her university professors. It had been James who had found her crying uncontrollably and for no reason that she knew of in a corner of the university library late one evening. She had wanted to die and she had told him so.

He had shepherded her to his apartment, where his wife, Lucy, had diagnosed complete exhaustion due to overwork and stress. Lucy was a sister at the local hospital. They had covered for her with the powers that be, labelling her condition a severe attack of the flu, and she had stayed in their spare bedroom for three weeks, doing nothing and seeing no one. Lucy had fed her hot meals, which she'd forced the patient to eat, brought her magazines and light books to read and refused to let her get out of bed. James had just been a friend, watching TV with her and cracking silly jokes.

It had been her first experience of real, genuine friendship from the male of the species, and she knew now it had saved her reason if not her life. She had been verging on a breakdown, and although she hadn't confided in James and Lucy about the Kirbys she had realised it was the years of frustration and pain on account of them that had brought her so close to a serious illness.

She had told herself, through the quiet afternoons in the peace and tranquillity of the Holdens' apartment, that she would rise above her past. She was not a victim unless she thought of herself as one, she'd determined resolutely.

After three weeks she'd returned to her studies and eventually obtained her degree, leaving the university but not her friendship with James and Lucy. That had continued, albeit from afar, with the three of them meeting up every few months or so. The last occasion had been at the christening of their daughter, Melanie Anne, when Holly had been one of the godparents.

Why was she thinking of all this now? Holly asked herself irritably, glaring at the stack of work in front of her as though it were the culprit. She knew David Kirby had died a few months after her brief stay with James and Lucy, and after that it had been easier to fight dredging up the past.

Christina, the Kirbys' foster daughter, had written informing Holly of David's death at the time, having traced her through the social services. It appeared David had tried his tricks with some young girls at the local youth club where he helped out, and when the police had started investigating the complaints Christina had come forward at last to speak of her own abuse at the hands of her foster father. The police had taken the young woman seriously, in view of the other complaints, and within a day or two—knowing his sordid secret was about to be revealed—David Kirby had taken an overdose.

David Kirby couldn't hurt anyone any more. His power over the weak and innocent was finished. And she was autonomous now, completely independent. Holly stared down at her hands, which were trembling. She could look after herself and she would never willingly give that precious and hard-won sovereignty up.

And Jacques Querruel? A separate section of her mind asked probingly. What about Jacques Querruel? This ruthless and quite extraordinary Frenchman who rode a Harley-Davidson with panache and didn't give a damn what anyone thought of him?

Jacques Querruel was everything she didn't like in the male of the species. Handsome, wealthy, hard and answerable to no one. A law unto himself. Intimidating everyone around him with his influence and authority. But he didn't intimidate her and she was not frightened of him either. He might be her employer, and of course she would be only too pleased to give a hundred per cent effort to this new venture, but if he imagined he had bought her soul along with the job he was in for a nasty shock. She would not be bullied or ridden roughshod over. Not ever again.

And if Paris didn't work out? She contemplated the thought before reaching for the papers on the top of the pile at the side of her word processor.

She'd cut her losses and move on. Simple. In fact she didn't know why she had ever got into a state about Jacques Querruel…

CHAPTER FOUR

THE short journey had been a pleasant one, but then with Jacques Querruel's secretary booking her in business class it could hardly have been anything else, Holly reflected as she stood waiting to be collected in the airport terminal. There had been a taxi to the airport too, all paid for and a handsome tip included, the cheerful taxi driver had informed her when she had tried to press money on him. It seemed Jacques Querruel thought of everything.

She would be met at the airport and taken to her rented apartment, where she could offload her luggage and freshen up a little, before her escort would bring her to the offices of Querruel International. There she would meet Jacques again and he would introduce her to the rest of the team.

All this had been explained by Jacques's secretary by telephone a few days ago and confirmed in a letter Holly had received twenty-four hours later. Efficient, clinical and unemotional. Unlike Holly's oscillating feelings.

The last two weeks she had fluctuated from being absolutely sure she was doing the right thing in moving to Paris to being equally sure she wasn't, her emotions seesawing violently, sometimes within the space of a few minutes. Her nights had been a mixture of disturbed, strange dreams—the sort she'd only had before when she was ill and feverish—and thick, heavy sleep that left her feeling more tired in the mornings than before she had got into bed.

But she was here now. She glanced down at the two

large cases and one small one which contained all of her clothes and shoes and a few personal possessions. And, with Michael Roberts refusing to even acknowledge her existence and his son taking legal advice, she wasn't actually sorry to leave England.

Margaret had told her on the quiet that Jacques had advised Michael Roberts that quite a few other women were prepared to stand up in court and testify that Jeff had sexually harassed them if it came to it, and that she doubted if Jeff would pursue any defence once he realised Jacques was absolutely serious in seeing the thing through. 'He'll go for keeping it all quiet and sneaking away to another job which his father will set up for him,' Margaret had said confidingly. 'But this time he'll have to keep his nose clean and actually work for his living. It'll do him the world of good.'

Holly didn't care whether it did or not. The whole episode had left a nasty taste in her mouth and she just wanted to forget Jeff Roberts and concentrate on the new job, which at the moment was causing the butterflies in her stomach to go berserk. She couldn't speak French; all the rest of the team had been together for years and years; she didn't know a soul in France and she had no idea if she was up to the sort of work which would be expected of her. And there was Jacques Querruel. Which was the biggest obstacle of all.

And then, as though her frantic thoughts had conjured him up, she saw him. Tall, long-legged and broad-shouldered, he was head and shoulders above the rest of the milling throng, and, as before in England, the energy and drive which was an integral part of his persona surrounded him like a dark aura.

She stood perfectly still as he made his way over to her, her heart in her mouth. He was wearing black jeans and a silky midnight-blue shirt, his arms brown and strong and his chiselled features appearing as if they were cut in granite. And Holly noticed that more than one female in the vicinity was giving him second and third glances, one young blonde girl, who couldn't have been more than eighteen, even going so far as to stop dead and follow him unashamedly with her wide eyes.

'*Bonjour, mademoiselle.*' It was faintly mocking and amused as he took in her rigid posture. 'I trust you had a comfortable journey?'

She nodded tightly, horrified at how seeing him again had affected her. 'Fine, thank you,' she responded stiffly. 'I thought—'

'Yes?' The black eyebrows rose enquiringly.

'I thought your secretary said a car and driver would meet me?' She stared at him steadily, holding the piercing gaze.

'The car is waiting, Holly, and I can drive,' he said with silky smoothness. He signalled imperiously and a porter appeared as if by magic at their sides as Jacques continued, 'Let us leave the airport with haste; these places are not conducive to conversation.'

Airports *and* Jacques Querruel, Holly thought with a trace of dark amusement, but then, as he took her arm and whisked her out of the terminal building, she ceased to think at all with the myriad impressions bombarding her mind.

Bright May sunshine, a crystal-clear blue sky, people buzzing about everywhere and the feel and faint delicious smell of the man at her side. These and a host of other things hit her senses with blinding impact.

She watched the porter depositing her cases into a sleek silver Jaguar before Jacques tipped him—handsomely, if the effusive quality of the man's thanks was anything to

go by—and then she was in the passenger seat and
Jacques was shutting the door behind her. As he slid into
the driving seat a moment later she felt her whole body
react to his, although she didn't betray this by so much
as the flicker of an eyelash. And then they were off,
sweeping out of the airport confines before she could
catch her breath.

'I was not sure if you would come.'

For a moment Holly thought she had misheard the soft
voice, but as her eyes flashed to the handsome profile he
glanced at her once. 'I had said I would,' she managed
quietly.

'Of course.' He nodded, and she had no way of knowing what he was thinking as she glanced away. 'And it is
a beautiful day to see the city of love, is it not?'

'A city is just buildings; one is very like another,' Holly
said from her vast experience of travelling nowhere at all.

'*Mon Dieu!* You are aware that such a comment is sac-
rilege to any red-blooded Frenchman?' Jacques asked
with cool mockery. 'Paris has a special magic, an *esprit*
that fascinates all who visit her, and passion is very much
part of this. It was passion that built the great boulevards,
the churches, the art collections and the reputation for
gourmet food. The French proverb, *"Pour être Parisien,
il n'est pas necessaire d'être ne a Paris, il suffit d'y re-
naitre"* is just as true today as ever it was.'

'Which means?' Holly asked warily.

'To be a Parisian one need not be born there, only re-
born there,' Jacques supplied silkily. 'But to fully understand this one must walk the streets and sense the life that
inhabits them, a life not only of the present but also of
the past. Almost every street has its trophies: a tree
planted by Victor Hugo on the Avenue Raspail, a doorway
in Belleville where the singer Edith Piaf was born, or a

mark on the Rue Bellechasse which records the height of the great flood. Paris lives and breathes, you understand? It has always been that way.'

Holly glanced at him, not sure if he was serious or not. And then she said, determined to not be overawed, 'If you feel like that about it, why is your château miles away from the city?'

'Ah, but not too far, you know. And I have my apartment here, so in truth I have not really left at all,' he said easily. 'Added to which my parents and sisters live south of the Latin quarter so the Querruel name is well-represented.'

'Is that where you were born?' she asked quietly, remembering the gossip that he had risen from squalor to riches.

'Not exactly.' He negotiated a sharp turn around a car which had suddenly decided to pull up without any warning at all, its occupant waving and shouting to someone who was obviously a friend on the pavement. Holly noticed Jacques was neither fazed nor surprised, and assumed such occurrences weren't uncommon. She decided she wouldn't try to drive in Paris.

'I was born a few miles from where my parents now live, but in Paris a mile can take you into another world,' he said expressionlessly. 'I wanted to buy them a château out of town when I was able to do so but they would not have it. They wanted to stay where they knew everyone, where things were familiar, I think. My father enjoys his game of boules with his old cronies every afternoon, and they meet friends for breakfast in the sidewalk cafés, that sort of thing. But they let me move them to a small house in a quiet cobbled street with a pretty garden for my mother to grow flowers. She was never able to have more than a small window box when I was little. They are content and that is the main thing.'

He obviously loved his family very much. Holly didn't know why that should give her such an ache in her heart region and she changed the subject as she said, 'I don't have to see the apartment now if you would rather go to the office. I'd like to start work straight away.'

'I think this would not be good.' He glanced briefly her way. 'We will take your things as planned and then we will have lunch. There will be time enough for work later. I am not quite the slave-driver you seem to imagine.'

Oh, dear, he sounded affronted. This was a great start to the new job—offending the boss. 'Lunch with the others, you mean?' she asked innocently.

There was a long pause. 'No, that is not what I mean.'

'Oh.'

She was about to say more when he pointed to her left. 'There on the pavement. You see? A gypsy circus.'

They had passed too soon but Holly saw the performing goat and two brightly dressed clowns, along with an organ grinder with an enormous hat for collecting money. She was enchanted, turning round in her seat to see more.

'The clowns keep a watch-out for the police,' Jacques said drily. 'They are all adept at melting away at a moment's notice, even the goat.'

Holly smiled; she couldn't help it.

'That is better,' he murmured softly. 'You smile so rarely.'

She stared at him in surprise. 'How do you know?' she asked boldly. 'You hardly know me at all.'

'Something which will be rectified in the coming days, I hope.' It was polite but there was an edge she couldn't place.

She nodded briskly. 'Of course. I'm looking forward to meeting all the others on the team too.'

He murmured something under his breath that she almost thought sounded like 'Damn the team', but of course she must have misheard. She stared at him uncertainly for a moment. She knew the company was situated on the Right Bank, which was the very essence of bourgeois respectability, and now she asked tentatively, 'Where exactly is my apartment?'

'A ten-minute walk from the office.' He smiled easily. 'And the Restaurant de l'Etoile is in the next street, so this means you will be at work once we have eaten, my eager little beaver.'

It was mocking and she was immediately on the defensive. She was here to work, wasn't she? He needn't sound so patronising about her enthusiasm. She frowned, deciding to say nothing more until they reached their destination.

It appeared Jacques was of like mind. As the powerful car nosed its way through the crazy traffic Holly became more and more aware of the big, dark man at her side as the silence held and electrified. His jeans were tight across the hips and his legs were long; he exuded a flagrant masculinity that was impossible to ignore.

She wished she'd worn a longer skirt. The one she'd decided on was a modest knee-length when she was standing, beautifully cut and close-fitting, but, seated in the low-slung car as she was, she noticed it seemed to insist on riding halfway up her thighs. Every time she tried to pull it down it slipped out of her fingers and rode higher. She wriggled a little, attempting another manoeuvre that would reduce the area of exposed flesh.

'For crying out loud, woman, will you relax?'

Holly bristled as her cheeks flamed. 'I beg your pardon?'

'You are like the cat on the hot tin roof,' he grated. '*Mon Dieu!* What do you think I am about to do to you in the middle of the day, surrounded by traffic in a busy thoroughfare, anyway? What stories have you heard that make you so nervous around me?'

Holly glared at him in a most unemployee-like way. 'I haven't the faintest idea what you are talking about,' she stated tightly, brushing her hair away from her hot cheeks. Horrible, *horrible* man!

'You mean you were not expecting me to try to put my hand on your knee?' he snapped irritably.

'Of course not.' She was truly shocked and it showed.

'I see.' His scowl smoothed to a quizzical ruffle. 'But you are nervous, yes?'

'Of course I'm nervous,' she shot back testily. 'Anyone would be, wouldn't they? I've just arrived in a strange country to meet people I don't know and work at a place I've never seen.' *And my boss, who has decided to meet me, is easily the most sexy and charismatic man I've ever seen.*

There was a brief silence whilst the formidably intelligent computer brain dissected the information it had been fed. 'Yes, I can understand this, but you are of the indomitable spirit, *n'est-ce pas?*'

'I am also a normal human being,' she stated sharply. 'Or do you only employ the Rambo types who know no fear?'

For a moment she thought she had gone too far. He *was* her boss after all, and her tone had been distinctly shrewish.

There was a longer silence and then he smiled, and humour was back in his voice as he said, 'The Rambo types I do not like, Holly. Of this I assure you.' He turned to look at her for a moment, the amber eyes warm and the smile still on his lips, and then he was facing the front again.

Which was just as well because she was incapable of doing anything but breathe, and even that was coming in gulps. Did he look at his women like that before he made love to them? The thought hammered into her consciousness. Because if so they must fall into his arms like ripe plums. Of course, it was all charm, and probably cold-blooded at that, but boy, was it good!

Jacques had just turned into a wide, winding road off the main thoroughfare, and they had only gone a few yards more when the car drew to a halt. A large modern apartment building with a pretty fountain set in the middle of a small square was in front of them.

'Come along.' He had left the car, was walking round the bonnet and opening the passenger door, but still Holly had to order her legs to obey the message to get moving. The car ride had done nothing to convince her that she had made the right decision in coming to Paris, but it was too late now. Far, far too late.

The elderly concierge sprang to attention as Jacques walked into the foyer of the building with Holly's cases, and it was clear from the tenor of the exchange between the two men that Jacques was known to him, but as the conversation was all in French Holly didn't understand a word.

'And this is Mademoiselle Stanton, Pierre.' Jacques turned and drew her forward. 'Pierre speaks very good English and he will be only too pleased to help you in any way he can,' he added to Holly.

'*Bonjour, Monsieur.*' They were about the only French

words she knew. She smiled and held out her hand to the little man.

The wrinkled and aged Pierre smiled back, his gnome-like face cheery and bright black button eyes warm. '*Bonjour, mademoiselle*. I am pleased to meet the friend of Monsieur Querruel and I 'ope you will be 'appy 'ere. I am at your service, *mademoiselle*.'

'Thank you.'

A lift took them up to the third floor and—Jacques having refused help from Pierre with the cases—the two of them stepped out into a thickly carpeted corridor which carried a faint, pleasant, flowery smell in the air. Jacques strode to the last door on their right whereupon he put the cases down and fished out some keys from his jeans pocket. 'Your new home, *mademoiselle*.' He offered her the keys smilingly. 'This one opens the front door and, as this is now your apartment, I think you should do the honours.'

As the door swung open Holly found herself stepping into a small passageway which opened almost immediately into one of the most charming sitting rooms she had ever seen. It wasn't large, but by making the most of proportion and unifying with shades of lemon and cream an elegance had been achieved which belied the flat's diminutive size.

The sitting room featured two floor-to-ceiling windows and a large alcove which provided space for a desk and bookcase, and the pale, muted colours emphasised the light and maximised the space as well as contributing to the overall sense of simplicity.

There was no door to divide the sitting room from the tiny dining area and kitchen, but with careful arrangement of the furniture each area felt remarkably self-contained.

Floor-length voile curtains waved gently in the breeze

from the partly open windows, and their colour was reflected in the two-seater sofa and two chairs covered in calico. A small balcony off the sitting room held a table and two chairs, besides pots of busy lizzies and camellias, and a tiny fountain in one corner which was making a gentle 'plink-plink' sound. This overlooked half of Paris, or so it seemed to Holly's enchanted gaze.

A bedroom led off the sitting room through one door and a bathroom through another, and these rooms were very much extensions of the rest of the flat with similar colour schemes. A buttery-blond carpet covered the floor in all three rooms, and the pale theme was lifted here and there by the clever use of shot-silk cushions in golden yellow and burnt orange, a bowl of fruit on the dining table, a tall, intricately patterned Japanese vase in one corner and other such stylish touches.

Jacques had positioned himself leaning against the wall of the sitting room as Holly had explored her small but exquisitely designed and furnished new home, his muscled arms folded over his chest and his amber eyes intent on her face.

'Well?' His gaze had been waiting for her. 'Do you like it?' he asked lazily.

'How could anyone not like this?' Holly said bemusedly. 'But when you said Querruel International would provide temporary quarters for three months I didn't expect anything like this. This must be costing the company a small fortune.'

He looked down at his Italian-made shoes, considering his reply. He had wanted her to work for him here in Paris and therefore he had deliberately offered her a package it would have been almost impossible to refuse. That was acceptable. He had done the same sort of thing before when necessary. He knew she didn't know anyone here or speak French, and therefore he had wanted her to be in accommodation which was safe and secure as well as pleasant. Again, this was acceptable, and nothing more than the duty of a responsible employer. However, apartments in this area were like gold dust and, as she so rightly suspected, extremely expensive. He should know. He owned the penthouse at the top of this building...

He really did have unfairly thick lashes, thought Holly as she took the opportunity to study him. His open-necked shirt revealed the soft black body hair which must cover his chest, and his arms were dusted with the same. He was easily the most intimidatingly masculine male she had ever come across, his wide shoulders and strong, sinewy body offering no shred of weakness.

He looked up and caught her watching him, and it took some effort of will for Holly not to drop her eyes.

'A small fortune?' He repeated her words thoughtfully. 'Money is relative, I think. An inexpensive place may provide all sorts of problems and then it becomes very expensive in essence, does it not? I know the security system here to be exceptionally sound. The inhabitants have their own key to the front lobby, of course, but Pierre monitors all visitors by an announced entry programme so they do not have immediate access into the building. An unfortunate requirement but in this day and age sometimes necessary.'

For her? Hardly. For a politician maybe, or some other high-profile personality. Holly stared at him, and then she said, 'But you walked straight in downstairs.'

'Pierre saw me approaching the doors and opened them automatically,' Jacques said smoothly. 'Therefore I did not have to use your keys. Or mine.'

For a moment the last two words didn't register and then he saw her eyes open wide as comprehension hit. He pre-empted any protest by saying coolly and matter-of-factly, 'I have an apartment at the top of the building, which is why I knew about this one when it became available just about the time you agreed to work in Paris. My secretary was saved the trouble of securing a suitable property, which was most convenient, and of course being so close to the company this place is very time-efficient.'

Her voice higher-pitched than usual, Holly said, 'I'm sorry, but have you considered how this might look to other people?'

'Other people?' The look on his face and the tone of his voice suggested she could have been talking in double Dutch.

'Yes, other people,' Holly reiterated tightly. Darn it, he knew full well what she was getting at. 'Folk are very good at putting two and two together and making ten at the best of times. You bring me over from England and then provide accommodation in the same building in which you live. They might get the wrong idea.'

Amber eyes surveyed her steadily. 'You have your own front-door key and so do I,' he said calmly. 'How could anyone misconstrue this?'

If he had got to thirty-two years of age without knowing the answer to that, she was Minnie Mouse! 'People talk,' she said stonily. 'They like nothing better than a good gossip.'

'Not about me, Holly.' In the space of a moment he had changed from charming, genial associate-cum-employer into someone who was positively chilling. 'Not if they value their well-being.'

'Maybe not in front of you,' she persisted doggedly, 'but I can assure you they *will* talk.'

'And this would bother you? That these nameless and

rather sad individuals might waste their breath in idle gossip?'

He was being deliberately obtuse here. She found herself glaring at him. 'That really is not the point.'

'That's exactly the point,' he said drily. 'And frankly the girl who stood up to Jeff Roberts and was prepared to confront me too is quite capable of squashing any prattle with one look from her beautiful blue eyes.' He smiled slowly. 'Look at you now,' he drawled softly, dark eyebrows lifting slightly. 'You are fearsome.'

No, she was not going to be charmed or sweet-talked over this, Holly told herself resolutely, even as she bit back a secret smile. 'I just don't think—'

'Good. Let me do the thinking.' As her eyes opened wide at his audacity he gave her no chance to reply, taking her arm and adding, 'We will talk over lunch, yes? I am starving. Would you like to freshen up a little before we leave?'

He was like a human bulldozer, this man! Holly stared at him, her eyes turning from sapphire-blue to deep violet. And arrogant in the extreme. No doubt he was used to everyone falling in with his plans—whatever they happened to be—for fear of offending him. Well, surprise, surprise, Mr Querruel; this little cog in the great Querruel International machine might just throw a spark or two.

And then he took the wind right out of her sails when he said quietly, 'Please, Holly?'

Now, why did he have to do that? she asked herself crossly. Speak in that smoky, warm voice which was more wistful than aggressive? She shrugged warily, determined not to let him see how he affected her. 'I won't be a minute,' she said coolly, reaching for her handbag, 'and we will definitely discuss this further over lunch.'

'Of course.' It was too meek and there was laughter in

his eyes. 'A good meal always makes one more reasonable, yes?'

She retreated into the bathroom with as much dignity as she could muster and shut the door very firmly behind her.

Lunch was in a delightful little restaurant built in a semi-circle around an open courtyard. Large glass panels slid to one side when the weather was fine, ensuring the restaurant was open to the sunshine, and the alfresco feel seemed very foreign to Holly. Unlike in England the menu was written in both English and French, and the choice was enormous.

Holly chose *salade de tomates et d'ouefs* to begin with—egg and tomato salad—followed by *poulet à l'estragon*—chicken with tarragon—and both dishes were delicious, as was the dessert, pineapples in kirsch liqueur. However, in spite of the beautifully cooked and served food, Holly found herself eating mechanically, every nerve and fibre of her being painfully aware of Jacques Querruel.

She didn't know how French employers treated their employees but she suspected it couldn't be *that* different from English protocol. And Jacques was not staying in the frame. Not that he was flirting with her—not exactly, she reasoned silently. It was more that he was acting as though she was an equal, a friend, rather than someone who worked for him. He was full of humour—something which hadn't come across so forcefully in England—and supremely interesting—something which had.

She was intrigued, she admitted reluctantly, which was a warning in itself, along with the unexpected quivers and the sensual stirring of her blood. And that was dangerous. She didn't want to feel any sort of attraction for him—or any other male if it came to that. Autonomy and control were the important things. And she had managed to live by their safe guidelines quite happily until Jacques had come on to the scene.

'It will be all right.' They were sitting at their table drinking coffee when Jacques spoke after a minute or two of silence. They had both been watching two little girls playing with their dolls in a corner of the courtyard for a few moments, the children's curls turned bronze by the bright sunlight. Holly found she rather liked the way the French seemed to eat out in families rather than just couples; there were quite a few children scattered about the place and they were all very well-behaved.

She turned to Jacques now, her voice enquiring as she said, 'I'm sorry?' even as she prayed he hadn't guessed how she was feeling about him.

'You are anxious,' Jacques said quietly. 'Which is understandable. But you will find the other members of the team are very easy to get on with.'

Holly finished her coffee in one gulp and put the cup down on the saucer, wiping her mouth with the linen napkin before she said lightly, 'I'm sure they are.'

'As am I.' It was faintly challenging.

Now, that she wasn't at all sure of. She nodded. 'Of course,' she said evenly, careful to keep her face expressionless.

'Of course.' He repeated her words in a soft drawl, his voice holding the edge of irony. 'Tell me, Holly, what does one have to do to break through the barrier you have in place?'

He rose without waiting for an answer, and she could do little more than follow him out of the restaurant after he had paid the bill. Once he had opened the car door for her and she had slid inside, she watched him as he walked round the bonnet. His black hair was so dark it had blue lights in the sunshine, and the black jeans and midnight-blue shirt sat wonderfully well on the big masculine body. He looked the epitome of the successful man about town—a film star maybe, or a devil-may-care playboy. Larger than life in every respect anyway.

'So, we now begin the ordeal by introduction.'

He glanced at her and she saw the amber eyes were smiling tolerantly. She wondered for a moment what his reaction would be if she spoke the truth and said meeting his colleagues was absolutely nothing compared to the last hour or two on her overheated nerves. Instead she merely smiled back.

'Let me run through a few names with you so that they will be familiar when you meet the people concerned. There is Gerard Bousquet; he is my production manager and you will have quite a lot to do with him. And Jean-Pierre Delbouis, Gerard's assistant. Chantal you have already spoken to on the telephone, and Auguste and Christian are two of the best designers in the business. They left very well-paid jobs to come and work for me in the beginning and I owe them much.'

As he continued to speak, going through the immediate team and then other relevant personnel on the fringe, Holly struggled to keep her mind on what he was saying.

They had barely discussed the matter of her flat at lunch. When she had raised the subject Jacques had coolly declared that there was no problem as far as he could see. He was rarely in residence at his apartment anyway—most of the time he preferred to commute to his château, some thirty miles clear of Paris, unless there was a work crisis or he was having dinner with his parents or friends in the city, or attending some function or other. Everyone was quite aware of this.

He had stated this clearly and firmly, and as the waiter had chosen that particular moment to bring their hors d'oeuvres to the table she had been able to say nothing, and once the waiter had departed Jacques had talked of something else and the moment to protest further had been lost.

Which might have been exactly what he intended. Holly frowned to herself thoughtfully. She didn't know. In fact she was feeling she didn't know anything about anything! But that could only get better…couldn't it?

CHAPTER FIVE

SURPRISINGLY, in view of all her doubts and misgivings, Holly found she took to the new job, her associates and the French way of life like a duck to water.

Her work colleagues were a great bunch on the whole, and Holly's only complaint—if she had voiced it—was that they to a man or woman openly revered Jacques Querruel. Only with the women there was an extra element to their hero-worship that set Holly's teeth on edge. But she could understand why. Oh, yes. Having worked with the human dynamo which was Jacques Querruel for eight weeks, she could certainly understand why, Holly admitted to herself one warm July evening as she strolled home through bustling Paris streets.

He was an inspiration, although she hated to admit it, and he never asked for more commitment or hard work from his employees than he was prepared to give himself. First in the office in the mornings and the last to leave, he set a pace which was as exhausting as it was exciting. Fascinating, mesmerising, hypnotic and wildly seductive—she had heard all those descriptions of the compelling magnet which was Jacques Querruel and she had to agree with every one. He was a one-off. A unique, inimitable being, a *sui generis* who was impossible to define and label.

Which made it all the more humiliating that she had ever imagined—for a *second*—that he had any designs on her as a woman. He had obviously been absolutely truthful when he had declared the reasons for taking her flat;

they had been ones of convenience and efficiency and that was all.

In all the weeks she had worked for him he hadn't put a foot—or a hand, or any other part of his anatomy— wrong, and, not only that, she had been forced to listen to the others talking about his extensive—and very active—love life.

Beautiful women were Jacques's forte it would appear—glossy, sleek, expensive consorts who openly adored him and worshipped the ground he walked on.

And why not? she asked herself honestly. He was magnificent. Jacques had been in the States for the last five days and yet his presence still brooded over the offices, impelling people to work just that little bit harder, stretch themselves just that little bit further.

She was just about to pass one of the numerous delightful squares which were dotted about the Paris streets, and now she stopped for a moment, her eyes idly following a group of elderly men who were occupied in playing a game of boules. Jacques had said his father was passionate about the game, and from the spirit of camaraderie in front of her she could understand why.

The scents and smells of a city summer evening were heavy in the air as she watched the gnarled veterans playing the old and popular sport, each player intent on getting as close to the small *cushonet*—or marker—with their own three steel boules as they could. There was a great deal of good-natured banter from what Holly could determine, the spirit of *joie de vivre* belying the men's ages, which must average around eighty if a day. She couldn't understand a word of what they were saying to each other but she found herself smiling just the same.

Music was playing on the street corner opposite the square—a group of outlandishly dressed students playing a selection of instruments to amuse themselves and anyone else who wanted to stop and listen.

Holly stood, the smile still touching her lips, and just drank the moment in. The sun was still hot enough to caress her skin with a languid heat and she brushed back her hair from her face, shutting her eyes for a moment as she exulted in just being alive.

When she opened them again Jacques was standing in front of her, his amazing eyes intent on her face and his lips curved with amusement. 'You see,' he said softly. 'The *esprit* of Paris is already working.'

'*Jacques.*' She knew she was blushing, which was so stupid, so gauche. 'I thought... You're in America.'

'Then perhaps it is only my ghost who is here with you now?' His smile widened.

She pulled herself together fast. 'I'm sorry, that was silly,' she said quickly. 'I meant—'

'I know what you meant.' His gaze ran over her face and the sheen of dark, rich, silky hair. 'And you could never be silly.'

She stared at him, terribly uncertain now. He seemed different somehow, she thought confusedly. This was not the dynamic tycoon or brilliantly intelligent and somewhat formidable business associate she had come to thoroughly respect over the last weeks. Neither was it the slightly distant occupier of the penthouse at the top of the building where she lived, or the darkly powerful, legendary socialite and womaniser who was reported to have a different lady on his arm every night of the week. But just who it was she couldn't quite pin down.

'I...I'm just on my way back to the flat,' she managed shakily after a long moment or two. 'Are you going to the office?'

Jacques's thick black lashes hid the expression in his

eyes for a second. She *hoped* he was going to the office, the tone of her voice had told him so, and now he cursed himself inwardly for revealing too much. And then he remembered the decision he had made over the last few days when he had found thoughts of her intruding at the oddest moments.

It was a ridiculous situation, he'd told himself grimly. He had walked on eggshells the last weeks over this woman and it was not going to continue. He had hoped she would loosen up a little and she had—with everyone but him. He heard her talking and laughing with the others sometimes, even Gerard, who was not known for his sense of humour, but as soon as he, Jacques, appeared on the scene she closed up like a clam. And it grated on him. More and more as the weeks had gone by. *Zut!* He was going to break through that reserve of hers if it was the last thing he did.

'No, I am not going to the office,' he said very quietly. 'I have just flown in from the States and needed to stretch my legs, unwind a little. You know?'

Jacques Querruel unwind? Holly thought of several polite and nonchalant replies which would fit the occasion, and then said, 'But you're not like that.'

'Like what?'

'You're not the sort of man who needs to try and chill out. You thrive on work.'

His eyes were clear, unblinking, his hard, firm mouth curved cynically. 'You think I am a robot?' he asked silkily. 'A machine? But this is not so. You cut me and I bleed like any other man, Holly.'

The mild, gentle tone didn't fool her. He was annoyed, and in retrospect she couldn't blame him. 'I didn't mean it like that,' she said uncomfortably, just as a great whoop and holler from the group playing boules indicated there had been a winner.

'For a woman you lie incredibly badly.'

Maybe, but then she didn't look on that as a failing. She had seen what accomplished lying by an expert could do when she was eight years old. 'I'll let you get on with your walk,' she said evenly.

'I walked this way because I knew it was the route you took from the office,' Jacques said quietly. 'I have an invitation for you.'

'An invitation?' It was wary.

He bit down on the sudden flare of anger and said smoothly, 'From my mother. I have spoken of the little mouse of an English girl who has come all alone to the big, bad city to work for me, and she feels sorry for you. She wants to feed you dinner.'

Little mouse? Holly opened her mouth to fire a machine-gun round, but then she caught the glint in his eyes. 'You're joking,' she said weakly.

'Partly.' A warm, strong hand tilted her chin and she was too surprised to jerk away. 'The invitation to dinner stands, though. She is hospitable, my dear mama, and she was horrified to learn that a stranger to our city eats alone in her solitary apartment.'

'By choice, I hope you told her,' Holly said stiffly. 'The others have invited me to their homes for a meal but at the moment there is still so much to learn that I study at night. And I like to get to bed early so I'm fresh for the morning.'

'Commendable.' He said it as though it wasn't. 'Very commendable.'

You bet your sweet life it was, and it was his darn company which benefited from her diligence, Holly thought aggressively. She intended to make a go of this job if it killed her; failing in front of this man was not an option. 'Please thank your mother for me and tell her—'

'You can tell her yourself tonight when you come to dinner.'

Had he listened to a word she'd said? Holly thought helplessly, the sense of *déjà vu* strong. Yet again she was in danger of being manipulated by this charismatic and extremely annoying individual and if he thought she didn't recognise it...

'Your mother can't be expecting me tonight.' She decided calm reason was the best policy. 'You've only just got back from the States.'

'I rang her *en route* and told her to expect us about eight,' he said firmly. 'She was very pleased.'

'But I might have been going out tonight.'

'Are you?' he asked directly.

She considered lying as she studied him through angry blue eyes but it was quite true what he'd said—she did lie incredibly badly. Nevertheless, just to assume she was ready and waiting to leap at his invitation was the height of arrogance. 'That's not the point.'

'You're right, of course.' He did one of the mercurial changes of attitude that had caught her out once or twice before, his voice meek. 'I ask your forgiveness, *mademoiselle*.'

Holly eyed him with dark suspicion before clearing her throat. 'I can't go tonight, not empty-handed,' she said firmly.

'You could, but if you want to take something my mother adores a particular kind of handmade chocolate truffle from a little shop in the Latin quarter, OK?' Jacques offered helpfully. 'We could stop *en route* if you like?'

She wanted to ask him if he was in the habit of taking

work colleagues or friends to his parents' home for dinner, but she didn't. He had made it clear his mother had taken pity on a stranger who hardly knew anyone in Paris, and, much as she didn't appreciate being cast in the role of little orphan Annie, she didn't want Jacques to think she'd made the mistake of regarding his mother's invitation as anything other than what it was. She knew this wasn't a date or anything personal. She suddenly decided she had been distinctly chary in causing such a fuss.

Jacques had been watching the play of emotions over her face with covert interest, and like the master strategist he was he knew exactly when to strike. 'So I can confirm she can expect us at eight?' he asked humbly.

Holly felt awful now. She nodded quickly, blushing as she said, 'It's very kind of her and I do appreciate the gesture.'

He could afford to be generous now he'd got exactly what he wanted. Jacques smiled gently, his voice soothing as he said, 'I know that, Holly. It was just that I surprised you, *n'est-ce pas*? But this will give my mother pleasure; she will enjoy having another duckling to fuss over. She is longing for the day she is presented with her first grandchild, but to date my sisters seem to be in no hurry to oblige.'

And he clearly hadn't even considered the notion of settling down. Obviously he was having too good a time playing the field. The thought grated although she knew it shouldn't have.

'So we will go home and dress up, yes?' To her dismay Holly found her arm tucked through his in the next moment and then they were walking together along the dusty pavements.

Ridiculously she found she had forgotten how to put one foot in front of the other, the strange, prickly sensations running up and down her spine causing her almost to stumble. She was overwhelmingly aware of the bulk of him at her side, the feel of a hard male thigh and his considerable height taking her breath away.

Momentary panic gave way to shaky pleasure as Jacques continued to walk along without making any effort to pull her closer or touch her more intimately. Holly wondered—with a faint touch of hysteria—what he would say if she told him this was the first time she had strolled with a man on a sunny summer's evening. Laugh his head off, most likely. Or pin her with one of those lethal, laser-type glances that he used so effectively in the business world. She had seen him cut an adversary to pieces without saying a word.

David Kirby had been able to do that. Most of the time he had been winsome and charming, using his clean-cut good looks and warm, pleasant manner to maximum advantage, but she had seen him reduce Cassie to tears on more than one occasion and without saying a word. He had specialised in cold silences too, when one of them had annoyed him in some way, demanding that the offender grovel before he would communicate with them again.

'Holly?'

As she lifted her eyes to Jacques's face she saw he was staring down at her with a strangely tight expression, and she realised he must have said something and she hadn't heard a word.

'What is it? What's the matter?' He stopped, turning her to face him with his hands on her shoulders, and she wasn't to know the look on her face had appalled him. 'Is it meeting everyone tonight—?'

'No, no.' She interrupted him quickly, her face scarlet.

'Then what? You looked...' He couldn't find a word to describe what he had seen.

Holly continued to stare up at him, angry with herself that she had let her guard down and allowed thoughts of David Kirby to intrude even for a moment. She felt a strange warmth at his concern but at the same time she wanted to run a mile. 'I...I was just thinking of someone,' she said at last. 'Someone in the past.' She moved restlessly but he didn't take the hint and let go of her.

'A man?'

His voice was different somehow and she suddenly felt trapped. He had moved her against the wall of a building as they had stopped, and she was expecting to feel the distaste and panicky fright she always felt if a male got a little too close but it didn't come. Instead her agitation was more in response to the way her body was reacting to the smell and feel of his. She had never felt the powerful enchantment of desire before but she was feeling it now.

Mainly because she was so tied up with how she was feeling, she answered without considering her words, her voice shaky as she whispered, 'Yes, a man.'

'He hurt you.'

'Yes.'

'Is it over?'

'What?' Too late she realised where the conversation had led. He thought she'd been speaking about a romance she'd had; a lover.

'I said, is it over?' he repeated quietly. 'In your heart as well as every other way?'

'Yes, it's over.' Her stomach was doing cartwheels but she lifted her chin in the familiar gesture of defiance he had come to recognise as she added, 'And I really don't want to talk about it.'

Jacques expelled a silent breath. Mystery sat on this woman in illusive veils that appeared as soft and gentle as silk but in reality were cold, hard sheet metal. He stepped back a pace from her, his voice casual as he said, 'That is fine, Holly, but the offer of a shoulder is always available. I will not say that talking about a difficulty or a heartache always makes it better because I do not concede to the "trouble shared is a trouble halved" kind of thinking, but sometimes it helps to clear one's mind of dross. Now, when you meet my sisters you will find, unfortunately, that within ten minutes you will receive their life stories, which are singularly unremarkable...'

He continued talking along this line as she fell into step beside him again, his voice easy and relaxed and his manner reassuringly nonchalant, and by the time they reached the apartment block Holly was telling herself she had overreacted to what had been nothing more than friendly observation on Jacques's part. He wasn't interested in her past life one way or the other; he'd just been making conversation on a warm summer's night, that was all.

Holly showered the stickiness of a working day away before washing her hair and quickly blow-drying it into a smooth bob once she was alone in the sanctuary of her little apartment.

Jacques had spoken about dressing up so she assumed this was not a casual jeans and top evening, but she didn't want to look overdressed either. She decided on a pretty khaki-flowered wrap-over top and cream pencil skirt she'd bought the week before in a wonderful little shop near the Rue Mouffetard, one of the oldest street markets in Paris, teaming it with strappy cream sandals and a short-sleeved cashmere cardigan. She was back down in the lobby within twenty minutes but Jacques was already waiting for her, chatting idly to Pierre as he did so.

She was relieved to see from his attire of charcoal trousers and open-necked pale-blue silk shirt that she'd got the mix of smart-casual about right, and his eyes complimented her even before he said softly, 'Prompt as well as spectacularly lovely. You are quite a find, Mademoiselle Stanton.'

'Thank you,' she said lightly, before turning to Pierre and smiling warmly at the old man. 'It's a beautiful evening, Pierre.'

They left the building amid further pleasantries but on the drive to his parents' home Jacques said very little, which made Holly even more nervous, all her senses tuned in with unbearable sensitivity to the big, dark man at her side. She pretended an interest in the changing scene outside the Jaguar's windows as she mentally rehearsed several opening lines of conversation with Jacques's family, and when they stopped to buy the chocolate for his mother she was annoyed to find her hands were shaking slightly as she passed the money to the shop's proprietor.

When they arrived at the small stone house in a quiet cobbled street south of the Latin quarter there were children playing outside open doors, old couples sitting in wicker chairs on their doorsteps, enjoying the warmth of the dying sun, and a general air of tranquil benevolence in the heavy air.

Holly liked Jacques's parents immediately. Marc Querruel was tall, like his son, and Jacques had inherited his father's handsome, faintly autocratic features and thick head of hair, although the older man's was now white.

Camille, Jacques's mother, was small in contrast, with dark eyes and hair that only held the odd suggestion of silver, and her two daughters, Josephine and Barbe, had followed their mother's build. They were all attractive but not beautiful, their aquiline noses being too strong on female faces to qualify them for such a title, but the two girls, like their mother, were perfectly groomed and possessed of a happy self-confidence Holly found herself envying as the evening progressed.

The house itself was a jumble of whimsical, rustic antiques and traditional country colours which filled every room with faded elegance and decorative flair, and it was clear it was very much a family home. Holly loved it. The big, exposed beams; plainly painted white walls covered with pictures and mirrors; and the splashes of bright colour among the gentle vintage fabrics and abundance of plants and baskets of fresh and dried flowers were charming as well as homely.

They ate dinner sitting at an iron and scrollwork table in the secluded garden, which was a lush haven burgeoning with heady aromas from the rich foliage, and the full-bodied, fruity, deep red wine Jacques had brought perfectly complemented the delicious meal that seemed to last for ever.

Jacques was expansive and lazily amusing, and for the first time since Holly had known him she found herself daring to really relax and enjoy herself. His sisters were fun and at times a little shocking, although Holly got the impression the two girls liked to create a little consternation now and again, not least with their handsome brother. He was quite protective of them, Holly noted with a little pang in her heart region as she listened to the two young women teasing Jacques about their latest beaux. Even a little old-fashioned.

This last Barbe picked up on in answer to a comment from her brother regarding the number of young men she'd seen recently. 'You are one to talk!' Barbe slanted midnight-black eyes at her handsome sibling. 'Or are you going to argue the typical male chauvinist approach? A man can do whatever he likes and he is just a bit of a rogue, whereas a woman who has a few partners is labelled a tart?'

'Barbe!' Camille cast a quick look at Holly as she said drily, 'Gone are the days when I could pack them off to bed for speaking out of turn at the dinner table.'

'It's all right.' Holly grinned at the unrepentant Barbe. 'And I agree, there's still some way to go before women have full equality in certain areas.'

'There, you see? Holly agrees with me!' Barbe eyed her scowling brother slyly. 'Men like you are the worst sort of hypocrites, you know; one law for yourselves and one for the female of the species. Don't you ever consider the fact that all your women probably have fathers and brothers who think about them the way you think about me and Josephine?'

Jacques looked as if he was ready to explode but before he could say a word they heard a voice calling from within the house, and the next moment a couple of Marc and Camille's age appeared at the open French windows leading into the garden. By the time more chairs had been found and the couple had joined them with a glass of wine and a bowl of Camille's superb custard-cream flan, an uneasy harmony had settled again, although from the murderous glances Jacques continued to send his youngest sister Holly suspected Barbe was not forgiven.

Just before the party came to a close at the end of the evening, Barbe leant across to Holly and whispered in her ear, 'Take no notice of what I said, Holly. I was only trying to annoy Jacques earlier. You must be different. He hasn't brought anyone else home before.'

'Oh, it's not like that, really.' Holly was horrified. 'I just work for him, that's all, and your mother heard I was a stranger in town and invited me for a meal.'

Barbe raised worldly eyebrows, her face saying volumes before she drawled, 'My mistake. Well, in that case, Josephine and I must take you out with us now and again, yes? Introduce you around.'

Holly smiled politely. Barbe and Josephine were good company and vivacious, and an evening spent with them would certainly be one to remember, but she had no intention of accepting Barbe's invitation. Before she could make this clear, however, Barbe had turned her attention to Jacques, who had just finished talking to the couple who had joined them earlier. Whatever his sister said in rapid French turned his handsome face dark and, after one clipped sentence in his mother tongue that caused Barbe to sit back in her seat with her mouth closed, Jacques rose to his feet.

'It is time for me and Holly to leave.' He drew Holly to her feet as he spoke, his mouth smiling and his voice pleasant, but Holly was aware of something simmering at the backs of the amber eyes and wondered what Barbe had said to him.

She found out shortly after the effusive goodbyes when Camille and Marc made it clear they expected to see her again soon. Jacques drove the car for a short distance without speaking before pulling off the road at the side of a small park, deserted and slumbering in the soft moonlight. 'Let's walk.'

'Walk?' It was a nervous squeak and Holly heard herself with hot mortification. 'I don't think—'

'Holly, relax.' Jacques captured her fluttering hand as he turned to her, looking deep into her eyes. Holly was suddenly taken with a peculiar notion that she was floating, that she was weightless, that the only real thing in all the world was the golden brightness of his eyes. 'I need to talk to you, to make a few things clear, that's all. OK?'

'OK.' It was a whisper but all she could manage. Something had changed in the last few minutes. The easy, lazily amusing manner had been replaced by something else, something she wasn't at all sure she could handle. But at least he hadn't asked her to come up to his apartment to see his etchings, she told herself with grim humour as she allowed Jacques to help her out of the car. Not that Jacques Querruel would have such a crass chat-up line, of course.

The park was little more than a small area of grass enclosed by mature trees, and couldn't have measured more than a few hundred yards, but there were a couple of wooden benches alongside the quietly tinkling fountain in the middle of it, and it was to one of these that Jacques drew her.

As they sat down he half turned to face her, one arm draped along the seat at the back of her and the other hand raising her chin so he could look into her eyes. Holly couldn't believe that she was here, that she had allowed him to coerce her into such a vulnerable position, and yet… She forced herself to reflect honestly. He hadn't had to use much persuasion, she admitted silently. She was twenty-five years old and she had never been kissed by a man, and since the first moment she had laid eyes on Jacques nearly three months ago she had wondered what it would be like to feel that hard, stern, sexy mouth on hers. And in a weird sort of way, despite all her fears and nervousness around him, it was a relief to know she could actually feel hotly attracted to a member of the opposite sex. Because she did. To Jacques Querruel she did.

He gave her a long, silent look. 'You might not like what I am about to say,' he said softly, surprising her.

She was trembling inside and praying it wouldn't become obvious to those devastatingly piercing eyes. 'Oh?'

'I told Barbe there is no way she and Josephine are going to introduce you to all the local young bloods,' he said very quietly. 'I told her that I like you. I like you very much.'

She was drowning in the amber light now, and as he took her face between his hands she shivered.

'Do you understand what I am saying, Holly?' he asked, still in the soft, gentle voice. 'I want you and I do not share what is mine.'

Too much was happening too fast, and yet it wasn't fast, not really. She had always known this would happen one day and now that it had she was amazed to find she was surprised he had waited so long before making a move. Oh, she was a mess, such a mess inside, she thought desperately. He had no idea…

'Do you like me, Holly?' he asked, watching the play of emotion in the large blue eyes staring up at him, eyes that were as clear and beautiful as the still blue lake back at his château, and just as unfathomable.

'It…it's not a question of liking.' She found her voice somehow but he wouldn't let go of her face when she tried to glance away.

'Yes, it is. I have been patient but this is not an attribute I embrace easily,' he admitted, his mouth twisting. 'My mother was fond of preaching *"Petit à petit l'oiseau fait son nid"* when I was growing up—little by little the bird builds his nest—but I see no merit in this.'

She tried to pull away again, forcing a harsher note into her voice as she said, 'You see, you want, you take? Is that it?' She had to break the intimacy; it was terrifying.

She had expected a denial but instead he nodded, his face moving closer, and then his lips were on hers. It was not a tentative or apologetic kiss but one of definite intent, his mouth closing over hers as though it had a perfect right to do so.

Holly's heart was thudding but there was none of the repugnance she had been frightened she might feel as imagination became reality; instead a sweet thrill of excitement and pleasure quivered down her spine, and her mouth responded like a bud opening under soft summer rain.

His arms were holding her firmly but not intimidatingly as his lips moved over hers, his experience very obvious as he encouraged her gently into more and more intimacy. Holly was enchanted, this first kiss as an adult everything she would have wished it to be. His lips were firm and warm and the delicious smell of him was all about her, his body hard and muscled as he moved her further into him.

For a few mesmerising moments Holly found herself in a strange world of sensuous delight, an alien place she had never visited before but which was full of wonder and sweet body stirrings that told her she was not an oddity, or frigid, or any of the other negative things she had been scared of. She was being kissed and it was wonderful, natural...

When finally Jacques raised his head Holly felt giddy and breathless, and his voice was low and unusually husky as he murmured, 'I knew how you would taste; I have always known. Like warm, sweet honey. You are very beautiful, *chérie,* and very kissable. Soft, tantalisingly soft; a sweet torment that could drive a man mad...'

He kissed her again, moving all over her face in burning little nuzzling caresses before his mouth moved to her throat, causing her to arch against him. 'Mmm,' he sighed softly. 'You smell good, you feel good.'

She had to stop this. She wasn't quite sure why—her brain had scrambled and was advising her that caution and inhibition were nasty words—but she knew she had to stop this. It couldn't lead anywhere; Jacques was the original wolf and he wasn't even in sheep's clothing.

'I've wanted to do this—hold you, kiss you—since we met, do you know that, *petite*? I want to undress you, to kiss you until you melt like wax in my arms, to take you to a place where no other lover has taken you before—'

His words hit her like a physical blow and she reacted in much the same way; jerking away from him with enough force to almost send herself flying off the edge of the bench if Jacques hadn't caught her first.

She shrugged off his hands, rising to her feet as she said shakily, 'I want to go now. I want to go back.'

'What is it?' He had risen with her, his handsome face intent. 'What is the matter?'

Holly couldn't move, couldn't even avert her gaze from his. She felt she was incapable of making a sound.

'Is it this man you knew before? This man who hurt you so badly? Tell me about him. What sort of man was he?'

'What?' She stared at him as though he was mad.

'You say you have forgotten him but I do not think so,' Jacques said softly. 'Do you still love him? Is that it?'

The shock and revulsion on her face told him he was on the wrong track and he mentally cursed himself, before saying quietly, 'What is it, Holly? What went wrong?'

How could she tell him? How could she tell anyone? She had tried once and it had been horrific. He might be disgusted. He would think that somehow, in some way, she had encouraged what had happened. She had thought that for years, so why wouldn't he? If she didn't tell him he couldn't despise her. 'I want to go.'

'He has damaged you? This man?' He wasn't letting up and she felt a sense of panic that was indescribable. 'Was he violent, is that it? Abusive?' he asked gently, very gently.

She swallowed hard, trying to keep a check on her emotions whilst deciding what do say. But her brain was dead. She felt stupid, numb. She forced herself to say, 'It was a long time ago and I don't want to talk about it.'

'That is a mistake.'

'How on earth would you know?' The words had come from the pit of her stomach and even to her own ears they sounded harsh and guttural.

She had seen the amber eyes widen and knew how she must have registered on his senses, but he stood before her without saying anything more, observing her in a silence that was more oppressive than any ranting and raving. 'Look, it's not what you think.'

'How do you know what I think, Holly?' he asked very softly.

She didn't. It was true, she didn't. Sudden anger leaped up inside her. She was nothing to him in the overall run of things. He was a man who was used to clicking his fingers and having a dozen women fighting over the chance to be in his bed; she'd heard enough gossip to know that at least some of it must be based on fact. She hadn't run true to form—she had been a little different from the rest of them. That was what his overtures tonight were based on. The hunting instinct. Caveman mentality. Well, he could go and... 'I want to go back. Do I have to walk home or are you taking me in the car?' she asked with icy intent.

Jacques said nothing for a full ten seconds and the silence was so loud it hurt her eardrums. Then he drew back a fraction, his handsome face settling in rigid lines as he said quietly, 'Of course I will take you home, Holly.' He smiled thinly. 'Contrary to what you might believe, I am a civilised human being.'

She stared at him, utterly lost for words for a moment or two before she managed to say, 'I know that.' And she did, at heart. The problem here wasn't his. It was hers. And didn't she know it? All he had done was kiss her. He hadn't tried to force her, he hadn't been aggressive— quite the contrary. And she had reacted as though he'd tried to— What? Rape her?

Suddenly the past was so real she could taste it—could feel David's strong, cruel hands and his wet, hot mouth. She felt nauseous, her stomach rebelling against her thoughts. 'I'm...I'm sorry.' She forced herself to speak although in reality she wanted to scream and wail and shout. 'It's just that...I'm not ready for...'

She didn't know what she was trying to say herself, so it was all the more surprising when his whole countenance changed, and his voice was even but not harsh or unkind when he said, 'Let's forget it, yes?' His eyes held hers, very steady, very calm. 'We are friends, work colleagues. Nothing complicated, nothing heavy. This is acceptable?'

It would have been acceptable but for the fact that his very presence charged the air with painful sensitivity and a sensuality that was mind-blowing. She looked at him silently, her heart contracting. She should never have come to Paris. Never have worked for him. Never had accepted the invitation to his parents' home... 'Yes, that is acceptable,' she said tonelessly. 'That is quite acceptable.'

CHAPTER SIX

JULY departed in a blaze of hot sunshine but August was ushered in on the crest of an even stickier month. France was in the grip of a heatwave, although with air-conditioning at the offices and in her apartment Holly found she could enjoy the unusually hot weather quite comfortably.

She had been incredibly embarrassed and nervous the first morning after the visit to Jacques's parents' home when she'd gone to work, but in the event Jacques had been so impersonally friendly and concentrated on the job in hand that she had relaxed almost immediately. It had helped that he had left within hours to return to the States, the situation he had been dealing with there and which he had thought resolved having taken a sudden nosedive which necessitated his urgent attention.

That had been two weeks ago now, and—due wholly to the heartsearching the aftermath of that evening had produced—Holly had begun to make an effort to integrate herself into the lives of her colleagues. She had accepted one or two invitations to their homes for dinner, gone out to lunch twice with Chantal, Jacques's secretary, and Marianne, one of the production team, and had numerous cups of coffee and croissants or pastries in the sidewalk cafés both before and after work with this person or that.

Holly had found that, besides the enormous world of culture and entertainment in Paris, the city seemed to be preoccupied with food. Wherever one was, a sidewalk café wouldn't be far away, and every other shop appeared to be filled with some kind of delicacy—pastries, cheese, pâtés, sausages and wine. The average Frenchman's reasoning was simple. Like the other senses, taste should be taken seriously. Art for the eyes, music for the ears and fine food for the palate.

However, in all of the socialising, Holly was always thinking about one particular Frenchman who wasn't at all average. She was longing to see Jacques again and absolutely dreading it, and since he had been gone on the second trip to the States she had found he haunted her dreams and occupied the daylight hours in a way that was positively galling.

She didn't *want* to think about him, or about the aggressive sexuality that was both exciting and frightening. Most of all she didn't want to think about the kisses they had shared when he had shown himself to be both hypnotisingly seductive and sensitive.

It wasn't until after she had had time to think about what had happened quietly and rationally that she'd realised just how much restraint Jacques had employed. He hadn't tried to rush her or ask for more than she'd been prepared to give, and this from a man who was vastly sexually experienced and used to full relationships in every sense of the word. And after she had rejected his advances he hadn't seemed too put out or disappointed. But then, with all his other fish to fry perhaps he hadn't cared much one way or the other?

Holly frowned to herself. She couldn't figure him out and he confused her. He had said he wanted to make love to her—she hadn't imagined that—and yet he seemed able to turn his feelings off and on at will. She had worked closely with him as well as the rest of the team since arriving in France, had actually met his family, had been kissed and caressed by him, and yet she didn't have a clue what made him tick. But he fascinated her.

She frowned harder. It was an unwelcome truth, but she was too honest with herself to deny it. And if his kisses had been the most mind-blowing experience of her life, what would it be like if he *really* started to make love to her?

She shivered in spite of the warm, pleasant air, stretching her slim legs in front of her and settling herself back in the comfortably cushioned chair on the balcony even as she told herself she must start thinking about her evening meal.

She spent more time on the balcony than she did in the rest of the flat: eating her meals out there alfresco, reading, dozing in the sunshine at the weekends, or just watching the sun set in glorious rivers of myriad reds and golds until the sky turned to soft indigo and a violet dusk replaced the blazing displays.

She had seen small birds fluttering to drink from the tiny water feature in one corner of the balcony in the mornings, and since she'd bought some seed from a pet shop on her way home one evening several bright-eyed and cheeky little sparrows were now regular visitors.

Somehow, and Holly wasn't quite sure exactly when it had happened, this tiny French apartment in the middle of Paris felt more like home than her bedsit in England. Although she still missed Mrs Gibson and Mr Bateman, of course, she qualified quickly.

Thoughts of her friends reminded Holly she had intended to phone Lucy and James earlier. It had been a couple of weeks since she'd spoken to them last and she liked to keep up to date with all the latest adventures of her god-daughter. Melanie Anne was now a mobile nine-month-old, and the fact that the child could only hotch about on her well-padded behind didn't mean she wasn't into everything, Lucy had assured her wryly.

Holly actually had her hand on the telephone when the front doorbell rang. She knew who was outside immediately. If it had been anyone other than Jacques Pierre would have informed her first from his post in the lobby, although in all the time she had been in Paris Jacques had only visited her apartment twice, not counting the first day she'd arrived in France. Both occasions had been relating to a matter of work. Even when he stayed in the penthouse at the top of the building—which wasn't often, as usually he drove home to the château he had mentioned—he had made no effort to invite her up for coffee or a meal. Not that she'd expected him to, of course, she qualified hastily. Not at all.

The doorbell rang again, an authoritative ring that demanded attention. With her heart thudding Holly walked to the front door, refusing to admit that the churning in her stomach consisted of excited anticipation more than anything else.

'*Bonjour, chérie.*' He had moved away from the door and was leaning against the wall of the corridor when she opened it, his stance easy and nonchalant and his arms folded across his chest. He looked wonderful, and as always the amber eyes drew hers like magnets. He wasn't smiling.

'Hello, Jacques.' She was rather pleased at how even her voice sounded. 'I didn't know you were back.' *Keep it light and easy, as though you haven't been thinking of him every minute of the night and day.*

'Just got in.'

She nodded carefully. 'Did you manage to get everything sorted in the end?'

'Eventually.' He levered himself off the wall, stretching

as he did so, and she suddenly thought how tired he looked. It caused a funny little pang which panicked her more than any sexual desire could have done. 'Till the next crisis, of course.'

He smiled then, a slow smile that warmed his face, his eyes. Holly swallowed before forcing a smile in return.

'Have dinner with me tonight?'

'Tonight?' she said, taken aback more than a little, especially after the result of their last dinner date. 'I don't think that's a good idea,' she said at last. 'I thought we'd decided we'd just be friends? I work for you...' Her voice trailed away. His eyes were holding hers captive and she couldn't remember what she was going to say next.

'Friends don't eat together?' he asked gravely.

'Of course.' The exasperation that was getting to be a familiar feeling when she was around him made itself felt. 'I didn't mean that. It's just that—'

'You've shared a meal with quite a few people now; why not me?' he said evenly.

She stared at him. 'Have you been checking up on me whilst you've been away?'

'It is a crime to enquire if my newest employee is being made to feel welcome?' he asked silkily.

Holly didn't feel she could go down that road without Jacques winning hands down. She tried another tack. 'I *have* shared a meal with you.'

'This is so.' He moved, taking a step or two until he was right in front of her, so close she could feel the warmth and delicious smell of him. 'So share another, yes? It would please me.' Dark eyebrows rose in a dry amusement that told her she was being absolutely ridiculous.

How did this man always make her feel as though she

was behaving like a child? Holly hesitated. 'Thank you,' she said primly. 'Dinner would be very nice.'

'That is better,' he said approvingly, eyes laughing.

'I'll just change.' She gestured at the thin sleeveless top and jeans she'd changed into after showering when she'd arrived home.

'No need.' He smiled winningly. 'I thought we would drive out to the château; I've been meaning to show you my home for some time now.'

Right. She gave him a long, silent look before she said, 'As a friend, yes?'

He had been watching her with a kind of amused speculation and now he bent down, swiftly depositing a warm kiss on her lips before he said, 'Labels bore me, *petite*. Now, lock your door and let us have no more of this nonsense.'

The moon, like a huge opalescent pearl, was just beginning to cast its gentle light into the soft, scented dusk as Holly and Jacques strolled down towards the lake.

The meal Jacques's housekeeper, Monique, had prepared and served had been delicious, and the château itself was magnificent, a fairy-tale castle kind of place with turrets covered with green and red ivy and balconies ablaze with pots of flowers. It wasn't huge as châteaux went, Jacques had assured her on her tour of his home. Some of the old country houses numbered thirty bedrooms and umpteen reception rooms, which made his six bedrooms and four reception rooms modest in comparison, but the grounds were second to none.

Holly wholly agreed with him. The lawns were emerald-green expanses dotted with leafy mature trees that must provide welcome shade in the heat of the day, but it was the lake that was the real taste of heaven on earth. Delicate water lilies bloomed galore, their honeyed, waxy perfume heavy in the still air, and frail and beautiful dragonflies were skimming the surface of the mother-of-pearl water in which wild swans, crested grebes and fat ducks reposed. Tufts of forget-me-nots and other wild flowers dotted the boundary, and beyond the lake and still on Jacques's property a thick wood provided sanctuary to a host of wildlife.

There was a timeless quality to the air, along with the outlines of a row of ash trees silhouetted against the shimmering water, which appeared as transparent as porcelain.

'It's beautiful…' Holly breathed the words, glancing up at Jacques as she spoke.

His eyes were waiting for her, and as he drew her down on a gnarled wooden bench positioned under one of the trees the look on his face made her shiver with anticipation. 'So are you…' It was soft, throaty. One finger touched her mouth, tracing the outline of her lips before moving down to her chin and slowly, very slowly, trailing down her throat and to the soft swell of her breasts.

Her heart thudding, Holly watched him with big eyes, aware she was beginning to tremble but unable to do anything about it. An odd sensation had taken hold of her, a mingling of fear and exhilaration and excitement, and although he wasn't holding her or restraining her in any way she felt utterly unable to move.

'Holly. Sweet, sweet Holly…' It was half-sigh, half-whisper, and as he pulled her close to his hard, lean body his mouth came down on hers with an urgent passion that should have panicked her. But it didn't.

Her arms went round him and she responded to the kiss because now he was here, now he was back, she realised just how much she had missed him. The last days had been a period of limbo, of waiting, and much as she didn't want to acknowledge it the truth was inescapable. She liked Jacques; she liked him very much. Her brain wouldn't accept more than that.

His hands were moving over her soft, rounded curves, creating a tender urgency which filled her with unfamiliar hunger. His kiss became more passionate and the sensuous pleasure Holly was feeling was so alien, so captivating that her reserve was burnt up in the heat of it. She was hotly aware of the muscled strength of his male body but amazingly—wonderfully—it didn't fill her with panic or revulsion, just an exhilarating awareness of her own femininity. *She was alive.* She felt the pounding of her blood from the top of her head to the tips of her toes, a hot, surging flow which made her conscious of every part of her body.

'Holly?' His voice was like warm velvet, his accent so seductive it made her shiver. 'Do you mind me holding you like this, touching you?'

Did she? He had raised his head, his eyes burning on her face, and after a long moment when she struggled to find words and failed she merely shook her head.

'I want you, but you know that.'

In spite of the flow of pleasure she stiffened, and he was immediately aware of it.

'I'm not going to apologise for wanting you, Holly. I want you in my arms, in my bed, but only when you want it too. In your head and your heart as well as your body. Do you understand what I am saying?'

She drew away from him just the slightest bit. 'Full co-operation in the seduction game?' she said lightly, in spite of her racing heart.

'If you want to put it like that.' He still had his arms round her and she got the feeling he wouldn't let her move away any further if she tried. Perversely she did try and she was right. Her soft mouth tightened.

'Surely you have enough female company without bothering with me?' This time the lightness didn't come off and she was mortifyingly aware of it.

'Ah, I see.'

Quite what he saw she wasn't sure, but when he twisted her round suddenly and she ended up on his knee she gave a squeak of protest before becoming very still. He was looking at her in a way she hadn't seen before, and somewhere deep inside her trepidation and cold fear had her transfixed. David Kirby had held her like this, on his knee, so many times. And even before that awful, cataclysmic night, when so many nervous feelings and awkward, half-formed fears had come together in one devastating whole, she'd known she didn't like it. David had made her feel sick and frightened, panicky without knowing why. How did she feel now?

She wasn't quite sure but she did know she didn't feel afraid. As she acknowledged the truth she felt weak with relief, the trepidation and fear melting away.

'I don't want female company plural, Holly.' She was so close she could see individual eyelashes and the beginnings of black stubble on his square chin, and she had to restrain herself from reaching out and caressing his face. 'I only want you,' he added on a low note.

He wouldn't if he knew what she was really like. All the old insecurities rose up in a flood which so engulfed her she couldn't speak for a moment or two. And then she said, her voice lower than his, 'You don't know me, Jacques. Not really. You just see what you want to see. The outside.'

He was getting closer. Jacques bit down on the frustration and spoke quietly when he said, 'The outside looks pretty good to me but you're wrong, *petite*. I have known you for months now and I am a good judge of human character. I have to be to survive. It is what has brought me all I own.'

'Maybe.' She moved quickly, slipping away from him before she gave in to the impulse to let him kiss her again. This was crazy, stupid. What on earth was she doing? She couldn't begin an affair with Jacques Querruel. He was flirting with her and whatever he said this was just a game to him. She would be one of many such brief liaisons, and he would expect her to abide by the rules, but unlike his other women she didn't even know what the rules were!

'No, not maybe. Fact.' The amber eyes were regarding her intensely. 'You know, sooner or later you will have to take the risk of trusting someone again, however badly this man behaved.'

'Why?' She faced him defiantly. 'Why should I?'

'Because if you do not he will have won.'

'You don't understand,' she said tonelessly.

'Try me.'

She could feel her heart beating in her throat and it was the oddest feeling. She tore her eyes away from him, glancing out over the tranquil water and into the shadows beyond before she lifted her eyes to the night sky, gathering her courage. 'No.'

She would never humiliate herself by trying to explain what had happened. She had tried that once and she could remember the horror and disgust on Cassie's face as though it were yesterday. And when she had tried a tentative approach to one of the social workers involved in finding her a new foster home the woman had made it clear she thought Holly was imagining things. Just think-

ing about it now, even after all these years, made her want
to cringe.

'You are thinking about him now, aren't you?' he accused roughly. 'Did you finish it or did he?'

For an awful moment she thought she was going to
laugh a laugh born of hysteria, but she caught at her spi-
ralling emotions. He had no idea. No idea at all. But then,
how could he? 'I told you, you don't understand,' she
managed fairly levelly.

There was silence for some moments, the only sound
coming from a sudden squawking across the water as two
ducks had a brief squabble about who was sleeping where.
A flapping of wings and a skid across the water from one
aggrieved party settled the matter and all was quiet again.

'Come here, Holly,' he said, and there was a huskiness
to his voice that brought her eyes snapping to his face.

She knew she should go back to the lights of the château, to Monique bustling about and normality, but instead
she found herself moving towards him. He pulled her into
his arms and took her mouth hungrily, and this time there
was no restraint. And she kissed him back just as fiercely,
yearning springing up with such power it frightened her.
Something was happening and she didn't understand it.
He only had to touch her and she forgot all the reasons a
relationship between them wouldn't work. She didn't
know herself any more, not when she was around this
man.

He kissed her for a long time down by the tranquil
silver water, fiercely, hungrily, and then just as gently and
tenderly, as though she was something very fragile and
delicate that might break. His body was hard and strong
against hers and spoke eloquently of his need of her, but
although their caresses became more intimate and their

kisses more passionate he didn't follow through on their lovemaking as Holly had half expected him to.

When he at last drew away slightly his breathing was ragged and his voice wasn't quite steady as he said, with wry self-derision, 'One more kiss and I shall—how do you say—blot the copybook? I am not used to such self-restraint when making love to a woman.'

She had felt the fine tremors across his muscled back as she had clung to him and knew he was making light of it because it was the only way he could deal with it, and now she said, striving for the same dry lightness, 'You have been spoiled, no doubt. Dozens of adoring women only too willing to become your slave? Not always getting exactly what you want is good for you.'

'You are good for me,' he said softly, and there wasn't a trace of amusement in his voice.

She stared at him, the air charged with subtle, painful awareness, and felt something raw grip her. If only he hadn't been so experienced, so handsome, so wealthy, so magnetic. Why couldn't he have been an ordinary man? Jacques had had lots of women, women who would have known exactly how to please him in bed and hold his interest. How could she compete with that? She was such a mess inside, she knew it, and ironically meeting him had made her face that she still had big issues to come to terms with.

Sexually she was still as innocent as the eight-year-old girl she had been when David had tried to rape her; she knew nothing about love and life and men. Not a thing. She had cut herself off from any possibility of romantic involvement with the opposite sex to such an extent she didn't know where to start. All the normal stages that adolescent girls and boys went through had completely passed her by—boyfriends at school, kissing behind the bike sheds, fumbling caresses and petting in front of the TV when the family were out, or heated embraces in the back seat of a car.

She wasn't aware her face had been a reflection of her troubled thoughts, so when Jacques suddenly pulled her hand through the crook of his arm, planting a swift but possessive kiss on her half-open lips before saying easily, 'Let's walk a while,' she was surprised at his change of manner. 'I'll show you the swan's nest and the cygnets, although they are nearly as big as *maman* now,' he continued as she fell into step beside him, 'and the home of the owl who also had a little one to feed until quite recently, when he decided he was big enough to pack his bags and cut the apron strings.'

Holly looked at him in surprise. He was a hard, ruthless businessman, and even his friends would have had to call him cynical and obdurate. She hadn't expected an interest in something like an owl's fledgling.

'What is it?' He had noticed her expression.

'Nothing.'

He stopped, moving her against the slim trunk of an ash tree. 'What is it?' he repeated softly.

'Nothing really,' she said uncomfortably. 'I just hadn't got you down as a wildlife enthusiast, that's all.'

'No?' He smiled, taking the opportunity to kiss her again before they walked on. 'What have you got me down as, Holly?' he asked very quietly after a moment or two. 'Or perhaps it would be best—for my already battered and bruised ego, that is—if you did not answer this truthfully?'

She glanced at him warily. There had been the usual dry mockery in his dark, smoky voice but just a touch of something else that had a distinct edge to it.

He caught the look and surprised her for the umpteenth

time that night by laughing out loud, a laugh of genuine amusement. 'You are priceless. You know this?' he murmured when he had control of himself again. 'As my father often says to my mother, God must have sent you to keep me humble.'

'Keep you humble?' The comparison with his parents had caused a dart of pleasure and it was against this weakness she said primly, 'Humble is not a word I would readily use when referring to you.'

He swept her against him, kissing her until she was breathless and glowing, but when they resumed their walk Jacques began to talk and suddenly she was hearing some of the history which had made him into the man he was. Bitter memories mixed with happy ones—his disadvantaged childhood and the cruelty—intentional and unintentional—a prosperous society could inflict; his father's serious accident when Jacques was a small baby, which had financially crippled the family; his mother's fortitude and quiet bravery...

'My father worked for a furniture firm and a heavy oak dresser fell on him one day and crushed both his legs. My father trusted them when they said they would make it right, but instead they paid people to lie and my father never got a penny in compensation,' Jacques said quietly. 'He had no money to fight them in the courts and we were forced to leave our home and move to a squalid tenement. My mother worked all hours, as a cleaner, a waitress, whatever she could get.'

'But he walks all right now?'

Jacques shrugged. 'He suffers a great deal of pain all the time but he has learnt to hide it. He also has a weak heart, caused, my mother is sure, by the injuries he sustained. Each day he is with her she looks upon as a gift. He is not a well man.'

'I'm so sorry, Jacques.' She pictured the tall, aristocratic man with the shock of prematurely white hair and his small black-eyed wife who clearly adored her handsome husband, and felt heart sorry.

'The first thing I did when I made my money was to break the firm my father had worked for,' Jacques said evenly. 'They were an old family business dating back a century and were very proud. They cheated my father out of greed and selfishness and it cost them their livelihood and all they held dear, including their reputation. I was not sorry about this and have never regretted it.'

No, she could believe that. You would cross this man at great cost to your own well-being.

'I learnt very early in life that society despises the weak and helpless and only respects power and influence.' Jacques turned his head, the amber eyes sending their searching light on to her face. 'I am shocking you?' he asked quietly.

'No.' She paused. 'But I don't think it is as cut and dried as that.' And it was only as she said the words that she realised that a great, solid ball of bitterness which had been lodged in her chest for years was gone. 'There are good people in all walks of society who try to right wrongs and stand for what is true, but I agree it's a battle. And innocents do get hurt. The manipulators, the cold, conscienceless individuals have a lever the moral don't. But you can't come down to their level in the fight.'

'I agree.' They looked at each other for a second before he smiled coldly. 'I fought them fair and square without breaking the law, although at times I admit I was tempted to take a short cut. But I had the element of pride on my side, you see. Their pride. How could the son of a menial, a menial they had dispatched with less consideration they would show to a pet dog, win through? Impossible. So they thought.'

'You hate them.'

It was a statement but he replied to it nevertheless. 'I did once, deeply and passionately.' His dim, hard profile was thoughtful. 'But not now. Once the power and wealth that was holding them together was gone the family fragmented, fighting amongst themselves for mere morsels. It was not pretty. My family is still together and stronger than ever.' Jacques gave a faint little smile that held no amusement. 'To hate what you have conquered is a waste of time and energy, *n'est-ce pas*? Almost as futile as fighting against the power of love.'

Holly's throat was locked and she couldn't utter a word for a full thirty seconds. How could she have been so blind? She asked herself wretchedly as they walked on. *She loved him.* And he was right—it *was* futile to fight against the power of love, but how could she have recognised that emotion for what it was before tonight? Before fate had pointed it out so cruelly? She hadn't meant for it to happen. A man like Jacques Querruel was not for her. She couldn't be more different from the sort of woman he dallied with.

She was a novelty at present. As they walked on amidst the wild flowers and sweet-smelling wild mint, Holly forced herself to face facts. She hadn't fallen into his arms at the first glance like everyone else. She'd been reserved, distant, and it had attracted the hunter that lurked under the psyche of every red-blooded male.

'Stay the night with me?' His voice was soft, a murmur. There was a significant little silence before his voice came again, saying, 'It doesn't have to be anything you don't want it to be. I promise this.'

She took a deep breath. 'Is that the line you give every

female you bring here?' she asked with what she hoped sounded like light amusement.

Jacques said nothing, and when the silence became screaming she forced herself to look at him. His eyes were tight on her face and they were both angry and searching. 'That is not you,' he said grimly. 'Why are you pretending to be something you are not? I thought we had got past the games tonight. For weeks you have hidden behind the glib repartee and I have had enough of it.'

'I've obviously been annoying you,' she shot back tightly. 'I think it would be better if I went home now.'

'Is that your answer to everything? To run away?'

'How *dare* you?' She was so furious she could have hit him and it showed in the stormy blue of her eyes. 'I have never run away from anything in my life, I'll have you know, in spite of having plenty of reason to.'

'Prove it. Stay here tonight,' he said swiftly. 'Your own room if you insist.'

'No.' She glared at him, burning spots of colour in her cheeks.

'Why not?' His voice was low, all anger gone. 'Why not, Holly?'

'I don't want to.' She straightened her shoulders defiantly.

'Liar.' He had the audacity to smile at her before he turned, pointing to a high tree lit by moonlight as he said, 'Up there, listen. The owl. Can you hear it?'

She said something very rude about the owl which shocked them both and sent Holly scarlet with angry embarrassment.

Jacques's eyes narrowed and he gave her a long look. 'I'll make it easy for you, OK?' he said quietly. 'You are staying the night. End of story, *n'est-ce pas*? It is a thirty-mile walk back to the city and not one to be attempted in the dark.'

'I don't believe I'm hearing this!' she snapped.

'I do not believe I am saying it,' he countered wryly. 'It is the first time I have had to employ such methods to secure a lady's company.' Dark eyebrows rose in cynical self-mockery.

'I don't doubt it.' It was scathing. 'Normally they are queuing up, I suppose!'

'Lines of them.' He nodded pleasantly.

'There's a name for men like you.'

'Several,' he agreed cheerfully. 'Charming, irresistible, debonair... Shall I go on?'

He grinned at her as he studied her hot face, and in spite of herself a warmth spread through her that was nothing at all to do with anger.

'It is an old cliché and I hesitate to use it, but you are lovely when you are angry,' he said with outrageous satisfaction.

'You're right, it *is* an old cliché,' she said sarcastically, refusing to let herself be sweet-talked round. He was impossible. Absolutely impossible. 'And I can't stay here. I have nothing with me and I can hardly go to the office in what I'm wearing tonight.'

'I wouldn't mind and I *am* the boss.' And then his voice changed, the amusement dying as he said very softly, 'Can't you tell me about it, Holly? I've been around; I am no callow youth to be shocked by anything you say. And I am asking because I care about you.'

From feeling so angry she could cheerfully have throttled him Holly was now fighting back the tears. He looked tough and fiercely male and yet very tender at the same time, and she couldn't cope with what it did to her bruised emotions. She swallowed, determined not to break down.

For the first time in her life she was longing to be in a man's arms and have him take care of her, accept her for exactly what she was and love her in spite of it. It was scary.

Her legs were trembling and she knew the shakiness came across in her voice when she said, 'I would if I could but…I'm not that sort of person.' She would lose all her hard-won self-respect, her sense of self if she told him; she knew she would. He would be disgusted, he'd think about her differently; she knew it. At best he would feel sorry for her the way people did for a victim, and at worst he might wonder if she had done something to provoke David to act the way he had—encouraged him even. People did think like that sometimes. She had experienced it first-hand.

Whatever way it went, he certainly wouldn't view her the same anyway. A woman of twenty-five who had never had a lover, even a relationship? He would think she was an oddity, a freak, just as the social workers and all the people who had dealt with her in her youth had.

She could remember the first foster mother she'd had after leaving the Kirbys talking to the social worker when they'd thought she was out playing. 'I have to say we haven't seen any signs of the aggression the other family reported,' the woman had said in a low voice, 'but she's an odd child, isn't she? Uncommunicative and a little…worrying. Has she seen a psychiatrist? No? Well, it might be an idea. After everything that went on before she came to us one can't be too careful with other children in the family.'

'Holly?' Jacques tilted her chin so her eyes lifted to his dark face. 'You can't shut me out forever. I will not let you. I thought at first you did not like me, that there was no hope in us being anything other than working colleagues, but I do not think that now. I have held you in my arms, I have kissed you, felt you tremble against me. Your body tells me what you will not admit.'

'I…I don't dislike you, of course I don't,' she whispered, 'but…' Her voice had a tell-tale tremor in it and she paused, trying to gain control before she said anything more.

But then she knew he had detected the wobble in her voice when he said, very softly, 'Always a but and always this battle inside you.' He drew her against him so her face was buried in the warmth of his chest, one hand stroking the raw silk of her hair as they stood quietly there, all words spent.

She wanted to cry, more than anything she wanted to cry, but she knew if she once started she wouldn't be able to stop. From when she had first left Kate and Angus West and the family she had grown up thinking was hers in everything that mattered, Holly had felt she was on her own. She had to face and overcome her problems herself, she'd known that. No one was going to help her if she didn't help herself—the affair with David Kirby had emphasised that only too clearly. She had had to quickly become self-sufficient and independent where it mattered, in her head, or sink. But she wasn't spineless or a wimp, she'd discovered, and she didn't intend to sink. Never. She wouldn't give them—the David and Cassie Kirbys of the world—that satisfaction.

But sometimes, like now, she felt so very weary and drained of resources, so tired of appearing someone quite different from the Holly she knew lived inside her. She gave a deep, helpless sigh and then straightened, drawing away from him as she said quietly, 'Please take me home, Jacques.'

'No.' It wasn't unkind, just very definite. And as her

eyes widened he continued, 'You are staying. Separate room, but you're staying, OK? In the morning we will eat breakfast together and then I will take you to the apartment so you can change your clothes before we go in to work.'

It all sounded too cosy. She forced a resentment she didn't feel into her voice as she said, 'We are not at work right now and to be honest I resent you giving me orders. I'll do and go where I want, and tonight I want to go home.'

He smiled, but the amber eyes were curiously opaque in the patch of moonlight slanting on his face and the cat-like orbs were fixed on her in a way that dried out her mouth and made her heart beat faster. In contrast, his voice was quiet and even pleasant when he said, 'Nice try but wrong approach, Holly. I do not take orders either. Now, if you had tried the defenceless feminine approach—all forlorn vulnerability and perhaps even a tear or two...'

She stiffened, his tone instantly dispelling any lingering weakness his tenderness had produced. 'I'm not into "trying" anything,' she bit out tightly.

'No, you are not, are you?' His tone was thoughtful. 'Which makes you unusual in my experience of the female of the species. I might even say unique.'

'I don't particularly care *what* you would say.' She was angry, not least because of the entirely unacceptable feeling of loss now that his arms were not holding her close.

'I hope that is not true.' His voice held the edge of irony. 'But I rather suspect it might be. Whatever...' He took her arm in a completely impersonal grip which was more insulting than any harsh words. 'You are staying at the château tonight so at least do me the courtesy of pretending it is not a fate worse than death?'

She glared at him, refusing to be drawn.

'And, whilst we are on the subject, I do not intend that tonight should be the last time you grace my home. All right? Just so you know, *petite*.'

'Jacques—'

'No, not another word.' His voice was rough and suddenly she found she was wary of pushing him any further. 'The trial period is over, *mademoiselle*. It is decision time. I would like you to stay in Paris and continue in your position at Querruel International. What is your verdict on this?'

'Verdict?' She forced a smile. 'You make it sound like a life-or-death decision.' She was annoyed to find her voice shook slightly and hoped he hadn't noticed.

Jacques looked at her without saying a word, and eventually—after a full thirty seconds had ticked by without him responding—she said, 'I...I enjoy the work and I would like to stay, if you are offering me the job, that is?'

'Yes, Holly. I am offering you the job,' he said softly.

CHAPTER SEVEN

HOLLY catnapped the night away in the sumptuous guest bedroom, which was a vision of pale angelica and warm ochre, with walls painted the colour of summer leaves. Every creak, every groan the beautiful old house gave brought her wide awake and looking towards the heavy oak door, but the handle didn't turn and the tall dark Adonis of her troubled dreams did not materialise.

At five o'clock she gave up all thoughts of further tossing and turning and had a shower, standing for long minutes under the warm, silky flow of water in the luxurious *en suite* as she contemplated how on earth she had come to find herself in her present position.

But it was him, Jacques Querruel. She dug her fingers into her scalp as she washed her hair, massaging her skin with unnecessary vigour. He swept everything and everyone before him like some great bulldozer, she told herself aggressively. He didn't hear anything he didn't want to hear or take notice of anyone's desires but his own.

Desires… The word curled round her consciousness until she turned the shower on to icy cold to dispel the heat it had produced.

She wanted to be angry with him. She *needed* to be angry with him; it was the only way she could keep her love for him at bay. She groaned, lifting her face to the icy flow. She was mad, crazy, to fall for a man like Jacques. He would eat her up and spit her out and go on his way quite happily. Of course he would. She would disappoint him in bed; she would disappoint him in every way. She just couldn't do any of this.

She was shivering convulsively by the time she left the bathroom wrapped in a big, fluffy bathrobe which had been lying across the bed the night before. It smelt wonderful, lemony fresh and expensive. As no doubt it was. Every brick, every square inch of the place reeked of wealth and power.

It was too early to get dressed and so she lay down on the bed again, still in the robe, fanning her damp hair out behind her on the pillow to dry.

It would be all right. It would. Sooner or later he would tire of his temporary interest in her and start to consider the entrance of the next female into his life and, no doubt, his bed. A woman who would be perfectly capable of meeting him on his own terms, sexually, mentally and emotionally. Who would act as his hostess if so required, understand any business worries, talk intelligently about almost any subject under the sun and behave like a lady in public and a whore in the bedroom. Jacques's normal type—if office gossip was anything to go by. She had seen pictures of one or two of his old flames in magazines which his fan club at the office had showed her, and without exception the women had been beautiful, intelligent, accomplished and socially élite. Sickeningly so.

One, a ravishingly lovely redhead, had been the executive managing director of her own company, and the other, an equally gorgeous blonde, had been a top model. Both formidably powerful women with brains to match. Of course. *Of course.*

She twisted on the silk coverlet, putting her hands over her ears as though the action would shut out her thoughts. She had to stop this. It was self-destructive and stupid, and she had never been either of those things until she had met Jacques.

She hadn't been aware of drifting off to sleep, so when she found herself surfacing from a thick, half-remembered dream and felt the firm, warm mouth over hers it took a second or two to come awake. And then her eyes opened and she was looking into his. They were very clear and bright, the colour of sunlight, and the expression in them caused her heart to stop for a second before it rushed on like an express train.

'Good morning, *petite*.' He gave her no chance to answer before he kissed her again, a long, drugged kiss, and some time during it he had sat down beside her, gathering her into his arms and adjusting her position so she was lying across him. 'I like starting the day this way,' he said eventually with a great deal of satisfaction.

'You...you're taking advantage.' It was a weak protest but all she could manage. Freshly shaved and with his hair still damp from the shower, he was mind-blowingly gorgeous, and she suddenly found herself wondering what on earth *she* looked like. No make-up and she'd gone to sleep with her hair wet.

'I have to with you. You do not play fair.' He kept his voice soft and easy, the memory of how she had looked when he had first come into the room still making his guts twist. Young, beautiful, untouched. He wanted her so badly it was tearing him apart, but the worst thing, the very worst thing, was wondering what torment this swine she'd got mixed up with had put her through.

He kissed her again, his hands sliding under the robe, which was loosely caught with the belt, and although she tensed for a moment she didn't push him away.

Holly's heart hammered painfully but after the long, lonely night of heartsearching all she wanted was his arms round her, his kisses, feeling him close and knowing that he wanted her. Not forever, she knew it couldn't last, but for now he *did* want her. Suddenly she wanted to forget everything else—the past, the future. There was only now, this minute, this second.

His hands had stilled for a moment when they discovered her nakedness under the soft towelling, but now as they explored the silky skin of her flat stomach before moving to stroke the soft swell of her breasts she began to tremble. Her arms had wound themselves round his neck and she was kissing him fiercely, hungrily, so when he suddenly put her from him and rose, walking across to open the curtains and then the windows beyond, she sank back on the bed in confusion.

'Monique will be here in one moment with your morning tea.' His voice was thick, husky, and as he turned to face her and saw the hurt and bewilderment she couldn't hide he said grimly, 'Did you want her to find us *in flagrante delicto*? I came to see you because I could not stay away, but—'

The quiet knock on the door checked his voice and brought Holly scrambling under the light covers in a whirl of legs and hot embarrassment, but when Monique bustled into the room carrying a small tray holding a cup of tea and a plate of tiny star-shaped biscuits the housekeeper appeared to notice nothing amiss.

Did all his women bow to discretion and make a pretence of sleeping in one of the guest rooms? Holly asked herself, even as she answered Monique's polite enquiry regarding how well she had slept. Or didn't they care? Did they allow Monique to bring a double tray to the master bedroom where they were curled up at his side, replete and satisfied after a night of love?

Before she had met Jacques the thought of a man's

hands and kisses on her body had brought a mild sense of panic and a definite feeling of repugnance, but now...now she didn't know herself.

Monique left the room after informing them both that breakfast would be ready in twenty minutes, and with the housekeeper's departure Jacques walked slowly to the door, a phantom of a smile on his face as he looked at her in the bed. 'I told you, Holly, it has to be with your head and your heart as well as your body,' he said softly, 'and we are not there yet. Neither will our first time be a quick coupling with the possibility of someone walking in on us.'

She stared at him, colour flushing her cheeks. 'You seem very sure there will be a first time,' she said as coolly as she could manage considering her limbs were still fluid from his touch.

'You doubt this?'

She nodded; it seemed safer. She wasn't sure that her voice wouldn't betray her surprise and disappointment that he was leaving. Which would be the final humiliation.

'I do not.' He studied her face, his eyes serious and very intent. 'There are some things which are as inevitable as the tides of the sea, *petite*. I have come to realise this. Once in a lifetime, if one is lucky, one catches a glimpse of destiny—personal destiny. The altercation with Jeff was meant to be. It brought you to my notice, and me to you, otherwise we may have gone on wasting time.'

There was no laughter in his face or voice and the whole conversation was weighty with something Holly couldn't quite get a handle on. She felt a deep sense of uneasiness come over her and it must have shown on her countenance because he suddenly was smiling again. 'Do not fret,' he said drily. 'We have time.'

'Time?' She eyed him warily. 'Time for what exactly?'

'To get to know each other better before we become lovers.'

In the weeks that followed Holly was kept busy—at work, as more and more responsibility was given her; tidying up her affairs in England and informing friends the new job was permanent; and seeing Jacques on a personal basis. The first two situations were a piece of cake to deal with compared to the third.

It wasn't that she didn't enjoy Jacques's company—she did, too much. And away from the pressures and demands of Querruel International Jacques showed her more and more facets of his complex personality, each one drawing her closer to the real man behind the powerful and successful tycoon the rest of the world saw.

They spent time together in the evenings and at weekends, sometimes going to the theatre or a movie or one of the fascinating nightclubs Jacques knew. Other times they just had a meal together at the château or went for a spin on the Harley-Davidson, stopping for a drink at charming little out-of-the-way places which Jacques seemed to find like magic.

Holly found herself telling him things she had never told a living soul. The insecurities, fears and pain of her troubled childhood slipped out more often than she would have liked in the light and easy relationship Jacques had woven. But she never mentioned David Kirby, and if Jacques tried to quiz her on past romances he met a brick wall. To admit Jacques was the first man she'd ever dated would have opened Pandora's box, and she could not have coped with that. However, she was becoming more and more aware that Jacques wouldn't accept the status quo for ever; he wasn't that type of man. Sooner or later time would run out.

Holly had accepted Jacques was allowing their relationship to progress at what he saw as her pace because he cared about her as well as desiring her. The more she'd got to know him she had come to understand he was a highly discriminating individual, the gossip concerning his love life exaggerated. He'd had lovers, she knew that, but she also knew Jacques would have had to like and care about each woman as a person. He wouldn't take a woman to his bed just because she was beautiful and had indicated she was available.

Jacques thoroughly enjoyed playing the seduction game but he played fair, although Holly felt it would have been easier to resist the slow and subtle invasion into her psyche if he hadn't.

When they didn't leave a nightclub or party until the early hours Jacques usually slept at the penthouse, but he never pressurised her to sleep in his apartment or in his bed. On such occasions she often found herself whisked up to the top floor to share breakfast with him the next morning, and that was fun. The apartment was a bachelor pad with a colour scheme of silver and charcoal and every modern convenience known to man, a technological dream. Utterly different from the warm, homely feel of the luxury at the château, but mind-blowing nevertheless.

And so the determined and persistent seduction continued, like the relentless drip, drip, drip of water on the protective shell of her heart, and summer faded to a crystal-clear and beautiful autumn. Holly found she was enjoying life in a way she had never imagined possible, but when the urge came to analyse exactly why she repressed it, refusing to acknowledge the unease which accompanied such feelings.

Since she had met Jacques there were times when she felt like a fully grown and confident woman who was learning to be at peace with herself and the world around her, then others when the past was so real she was eight years old again.

She could recall the frantic panic as David Kirby literally ripped the clothes off her back, the concentrated horror in her mind as she had fought him, twisting and turning and scrambling about the bed until at last he had given up. But not before he had left her with deep scratches on the tops of her legs and thighs, and bruises all over.

She should have made Cassie or someone look at the marks his lust had made on her tender flesh—how often had she berated herself with that thought? But she had been a small child—bewildered, scared out of her wits and horribly ashamed.

It hadn't been her fault, none of it, but it had taken a long, long time for that fact to become an accepted reality, along with the truth that Kate and Angus West had had no choice but to give her up. They hadn't abandoned her or got rid of her, although that was what it had felt like for years. She had learnt much later, when in her teens, that the couple had died within weeks of each other just three months after she had been taken away from the family, and so there had been the best reasons in the world why they had never made contact again or tried to see her.

But sometimes—just sometimes—all the reasoned arguments and rationalisation in the world didn't help, and the sense of aloneness would sweep over her with a fierceness that was consuming. And strangely that happened more often when she had been in Jacques's arms, when he had been kissing and caressing her with a primitive possessiveness which made her head reel and her body come alive in a way she'd never dreamt of. And every time he pushed the sexual boundaries just a little bit more.

It couldn't continue, of course. But when the final confrontation came it happened in a way she had never expected and wasn't prepared for.

'I want you to—how do you say—put the glad rags on tonight, eh?'

Holly was in Jacques's office on a crisp Friday evening in October and everyone else had gone home. He had just kissed her until she was breathless and trembling on her legs, her heart pounding, and the amber eyes were surveying her with complacent satisfaction.

She put a little space between them after placing the report she had been delivering on his desk, and then was able to say fairly steadily, 'Why?'

'Some old friends of mine are having a party and we're invited. Alain and Marguerite have heard about this little slip of an English girl with hair like raw silk and eyes the colour of cornflowers and they want to meet you.'

Her cheeks grew warm. 'You've told them about me?'

'Of course I have told them about you,' he said softly, very softly. 'They have been abroad for a few months with Alain's job but now they are back and anxious to see the siren who has captured my heart.'

His eyes were full of laughter, one dark eyebrow quirked, but there was something in the tone of his voice which sent warning signals buzzing in her head. He looked perfectly calm and relaxed, and there was no need to think his words carried any significance beyond mild flirtatiousness, but suddenly Holly wasn't sure.

But all this was just a game to Jacques, she knew that, she told herself silently. He was the original love 'em and leave 'em Romeo, a confirmed bachelor and man-about-town who enjoyed women's company and treated them well but never made any commitment. In all the time they had been dating she hadn't asked him if he was seeing her exclusively because she had not felt she had the right, but she had made it clear she considered their relationship one with no strings attached. Light and easy. No ties, no obligations. That way when he left her for someone else who could be everything he wanted it wouldn't be so bad...would it? And she had been obsessional about hiding her love for him, which just would *not* die a death. But that was her problem.

Holly drew in a deep silent breath before saying brightly, 'I think a party would be a great way to start the weekend. What time do you want me ready?'

'Eight o'clock?' His eyes narrowed on her face. 'But wait a few minutes and we'll walk home together, yes?'

'I've got some shopping to do,' she said lightly. 'It's best I see you later.' She had decided, very early on in her new life, to keep work and play totally separate in spite of Jacques's presence in both. Therefore she had made it plain to him that arriving at the office together or leaving at the same time was not an option. He hadn't liked it, he still didn't like it, but he'd played ball.

For a long moment more Jacques studied her face, his eyes searching. 'Fine,' he said casually, conscious that she then relaxed at the word, which made him angry. She fought him at every turn and there were times when he had come very near to forgetting every principle he held dear and using her own need and desire of him against her. And she did want him, physically. The rest he wasn't quite sure of. And he didn't like that. In fact he was beginning to think that maybe a mental acceptance of his place in her life would only come after the physical act had been accomplished and got out of the way.

His eyes narrowed still more as a sliver of ruthless excitement curled down his spine. *Whoever this man was, whatever he had been to her, he was in the past.* Where he would remain.

Jacques's nostrils flared, his hard mouth twisting as he forced a smile. 'See you at eight.' He lowered his head to the papers on his desk, purposely dismissive in both tone and action.

He had been patient for months and where was it getting him? Nowhere. Where words and reason had failed, action would prevail. He wasn't about to let this ridiculous situation continue any longer. He heard the door to his office open and close, and it was only then he raised his head again.

Perched on the top of a hill to the west of Paris, the tiny village of Montfort L'Amaury dated from the Middle Ages. As Jacques's Jaguar approached the tranquil and beautiful setting it resembled a Christmas card, the deep, dark, velvet sky pierced with twinkling stars shining down on the sleeping village. Lights were glowing in windows here and there, squares of colour in the dark streets, and as Jacques drew up outside his friends' large house a dog barked somewhere in the distance, the sound melancholy.

Jacques leant across to her before he exited the car, his lips caressing her cheek as he murmured, 'You look beautiful, *chérie*. They will be enchanted.'

Holly watched him as he walked round the bonnet to open her door. In the months she had been with him she had learnt to accept such courtesies as part of Jacques; it came as second nature to him to open doors for her, see she was seated before he sat himself—all manner of things she had found alien at first. She wasn't used to being looked after or cherished, and it had been difficult to take in such small but gallant civilities at first. And then she had realised it wasn't an act on Jacques's part. It was natural to him, as natural as breathing, and she had understood he had probably always behaved such. It was dangerously nice.

Once out of the car she smoothed her hair and resisted the impulse to fiddle with her earrings. She had made an extra-special effort to look good tonight although she couldn't have explained why. The ice-blue tux jacket teamed perfectly with her silver top and silver sequinned mini, and she knew that cool colours brought out the violet in her eyes and emphasised the richness of her hair. Nevertheless, she was nervous and she didn't know why. She had got used to meeting Jacques's friends and colleagues in the last months and this evening would be nothing unusual.

It wasn't. Not at first. Alain and his pretty, dark-haired wife were charming and welcomed Holly with open arms, and as more guests arrived Holly and Jacques drifted into the enormous sun room stretching out from the drawing room.

A pianist was playing in one corner—there was to be a band later—and large full-length windows looked out on to the garden. The trees were alive with fairy lights and lanterns and these illuminated the impeccably kept smooth lawn and immaculate flower beds, although Holly caught sight of a child's brightly coloured tricycle lying on its side amidst all the perfection.

She smiled to herself, the small touch of ordinary humanity was comforting, surrounded as she was by Diors and diamonds. She was still smiling when her eyes were caught and held by the startled gaze of a young woman on the opposite side of the room.

It had been seventeen years since she had last set eyes on Christina in the flesh, but David and Cassie's foster daughter had included a photograph of herself in the letter she had written to Holly after David had committed suicide. Holly had written a polite note back to the other girl but declined the invitation to meet her, neither had she included a photograph, but it was clear Christina recognised her nevertheless.

Holly found herself shrinking inwardly, as though she was shrivelling from the panic and rush of memories which the other girl's face had called up. *It was impossible.* Christina, here? In France? In this particular home? What was she going to do? *What was she going to do?*

'What is it?' She must have looked awful because Jacques's voice was concerned, his eyes raking her face as he took her arm. 'Do you feel unwell?'

'Yes...'

'Do you want to leave?'

Yes, she wanted to leave, she had never wanted to leave somewhere so much in her life, but it was too late.

Holly remained quite still as Christina approached them, a sense of inevitability numbing the panic born of shame and fright. Just talk to her as you would anyone else, a voice in her head cautioned silently. Treat her as an old childhood friend you haven't seen in years. Jacques knows you were fostered in several homes; he won't think anything of this beyond mild surprise at such a coincidence.

When Christina had written to her she had hinted that she thought their foster parent might have hurt Holly as he had her but that was all. She clearly hadn't been sure. And it wasn't something you could discuss at a party anyway. There was no need for panic. None at all.

'Holly? It is you?' Christina seemed genuinely pleased to see her and Holly felt guilty for a moment that she didn't feel the same. She had forgiven Christina and the others for lying about her years ago—they had only been scared children manipulated by an evil man, after all— but there were too many unpleasant memories tied up with the smiling blonde woman in front of her. 'Oh, this is wonderful! I can't believe it.'

'Hello, Christina.' Holly knew the blood had drained from her face when she had first caught sight of the other woman but now her cheeks were burning. 'How…how are you?'

'Very well.' Christina didn't hesitate as she put her arms round Holly and hugged her for a moment, but Holly felt as though her arms were fixed to her sides by super-glue. And then, as Christina stepped back a pace, her face alight, she said, 'Oh, it's so good to see you, Holly, after all this time,' before her eyes flickered to Jacques in a manner which made it clear she was waiting to be introduced.

Holly swallowed. 'Christina, meet Jacques. Jacques, this is an old friend of mine from England. We…we knew each other when we were children.'

'Really?' Jacques was smiling politely as he shook Christina's outstretched hand but there had been the slightest of pauses when he scrutinised Holly's face before responding. 'It is good to meet a friend of Holly's,' he continued smoothly. 'Was she as beautiful a child as she is a woman, Christina?'

'Definitely.' Christina beamed at them both and Holly was conscious of thinking—ungraciously as well as un-fairly, she admitted silently—that Christina couldn't be as thick as she seemed. Surely she could see Holly wasn't exactly over the moon about renewing their connection?

It appeared not.

'I'm so glad I've seen you.' Christina seemed to have the impression the sentiment was returned. 'I wrote to you again after that first letter, you know, but the university returned it with ''not at this address'' written on the envelope.'

Holly nodded. Actually, she had written it. 'Well, here I am,' she said brightly, recovering a measure of composure. 'And here are you. Are you with someone?'

'My husband.' Christina beamed the hundred-watt smile again. 'Oh, here he is. Louis, this is Holly. You remember I spoke of her? This is my husband, Louis.'

The tall, slim man with dark eyes and grey hair was clearly twenty or so years older than his pretty wife, but he seemed very nice as he shook their hands and made the usual small talk for some moments. Holly was just thinking it was going to be all right, when Christina took her arm, drawing her slightly aside as she said, her voice low, 'I've wanted to see you again for so long, Holly. To…to say sorry as much as anything else. Both of us, John and I, knew we should have spoken up and told the truth about you instead of endorsing David's lies.'

'It's all right.' Holly spoke quickly. 'Forget it.'

'No.' Christina placed her hand on Holly's sleeve and it was all she could do not to shake it off and run away. She was terribly aware of Jacques at the side of her, and although he seemed to be deep in conversation with Christina's husband she wasn't sure he wasn't listening.

'The thing is, David was so good at manipulation and control,' Christina continued softly. 'He was doing the same thing to both of us but we never talked about it, not even to each other. It wasn't until I was older and everything happened with the youth club that I spoke out. And then John came forward too.'

'Christina, I don't want to talk about it.'

This time even Christina couldn't miss the tone of Holly's voice. The other girl stiffened for a moment and then relaxed, shaking her head as she said even more quietly, 'I was like that once. Then with the court case my mother came forward—I hadn't seen her in years—and through that I found out my father was French, and through my father I met Louis. I could have missed that.'

'I've met my mother and I don't like her,' Holly said flatly, 'and my father was someone she had little more than a one-night-stand with who already had several children with his wife. I'm not missing anything on that score, believe me.'

'Holly, it really helps to bring everything out into the open.'

'Christina, I'm glad things have worked out for you but the past is the past—'

'Have you had therapy?' Christina interrupted her with all the fervour of a true devotee of the treatment. 'Because it really helps. I was so screwed up, but I started it after David's death and I still go along once a month now. I've got a marvellous therapist right here in Paris. I could give you her name if you like.'

Holly didn't know if she felt better or worse when Marguerite materialised at the side of them in the next moment, the Frenchwoman's face smiling as she said, 'I was looking for you two to introduce you but you have found each other already. It is nice to meet someone from home when you are getting accustomed to a new country, n'est-ce pas?' she added directly to Holly.

Yeah, terrific. 'Very nice,' Holly confirmed tightly, aware the two men had finished their conversation and were looking at the three of them.

'And would you believe we know one another, Marguerite?' Christina put in happily.

'No, really?' Marguerite's eyes were bright with interest.

'It is a small world, as they say.' Jacques spoke at the side of them and then, as he took Holly's arm, he continued smoothly, 'But there are several people here who have not met Holly yet, so if you will excuse us...'

Had he heard anything? Holly glanced at Jacques's face as they walked away from the others but she could read nothing from the implacable countenance. However, he didn't whisk her away to a corner somewhere and start the third degree as she had half expected. Instead he did as he had said he was going to do and introduced her to more of his friends she hadn't yet met, as well as striking up conversations with several she had.

He hadn't been listening to Christina. The sick churning eased a little although curls of uneasiness remained. Everything was all right. All she had to do now was to avoid the other girl for the rest of the evening if she could.

In the event it was not hard. Jacques steered her from group to group, smiling, making easy conversation and taking care of things in such a way Holly found she only had to smile and speak in monosyllables, which was just as well considering the state of her shattered nerves.

Of all the places in all the world Christina had to pick this particular city in which to settle down, Holly thought wryly. And what were the chances of her husband knowing Alain and Marguerite? Millions to one. But it was no use dwelling on that. It had happened. She had been in Paris months now and gone to several parties and other social gatherings with Jacques and his friends, and she hadn't seen Christina before. It was probable she wouldn't see her again. Perhaps Louis was an associate or friend of Alain and Marguerite but not Jacques or his circle? She hoped so. She would question Jacques later about the other couple, but discreetly.

Soft piano music had been drifting about the downstairs

of the house since they had arrived, but once the buffet had been served and everyone had eaten a band moved in. Holly had found she couldn't eat a morsel, her nerves stretched like piano-wire, but if Jacques noticed her lack of appetite he didn't remark on it.

However, more than once she caught him staring at her, and his eyes were more intent and a clearer amber than she had ever seen them before, but then he would smile his slow, lazy smile and she told herself she was imagining things because of the turmoil her mind was in. It had been a shock seeing Christina; it had brought the past alive in a way which left an acidic taste in her mouth, but she didn't have to panic. Nothing was going to intrude on her new life here. It was a fool's paradise and she knew it at heart, but she clung to the hope right until the end of the evening.

Christina and Louis had already left but the other girl had done no more than wave her goodbye across the room, something which had caused Holly a pang of guilt before she had told herself it was for the best. Her attitude might have caused Christina a little disappointment but that was all. And the alternative—of sitting and talking about 'old times' or resurrecting the secret misery which had been life at the Kirbys'—was unthinkable.

Alain and Marguerite hugged her as she and Jacques left, extracting a promise from Holly that she would come to tea soon so she could meet their two children, and then they were out on the drive under the starry sky and the nightmare was over. Or so she thought. For about two minutes.

Jacques drove the car out of the drive, along the small lane which bordered two or three large houses, and then pulled into a parking place which was quiet and secluded and overshadowed by the branches of several huge evergreen oaks. He cut the engine, turning in his seat and draping one arm along the back of hers as his eyes narrowed on her wary face.

'Cerulean.'

It wasn't what she had expected him to say and she stared at him for a moment before she said guardedly, 'I'm sorry?'

'The colour of your eyes when you are disturbed about something. The blue becomes very deep and strong. I have noticed this before.'

Holly tried to think of something to say and failed utterly.

'Who was David, Holly?' His voice was quiet, even gentle, but she wasn't fooled. Her time had run out. He wasn't going to be fobbed off again, she could read it in his eyes. 'And what was his connection with you and Christina?'

'You were listening,' she accused weakly.

'Not as much as I would have liked,' he said grimly. 'Her damn husband kept talking about his golf handicap until I was tempted to find a club and wrap it round his head. But I caught the odd word here and there, a couple of which I did not like.'

'Oh?' She gave him a quick glance, then looked away again. His face was inscrutable and giving nothing away. 'Like what?'

'Just little words like therapy and court case along with this man's name,' Jacques said tonelessly, the very lack of emotion in his voice revealing how concerned he was. 'What was he to you and this other girl? Did you both go out with him, is that it? And he treated you both badly? He had some sort of problem obviously. Was he abusive, physically, I mean?'

'Please, Jacques.' She couldn't do this; she just could

not *do* this. She loved him so much but she wasn't what he thought she was. Inside she was such a mess, so mixed up and confused. He had no idea how terrified she was about loving him, of letting herself become vulnerable, open. And what would be a huge life-or-death type experience for her wouldn't mean the same to him. Sooner or later their affair would end and then what would she do? It was bad enough now to contemplate life without him, but if she gave herself to him, body and soul…

'No, enough! No more "please, Jacques",' he said harshly, so harshly her eyes shot to his face again. 'It is always like this, Holly. There are so many things that do not make sense, so many minefields where you are concerned. I do not understand what you want from me. If it had been any other woman I would have been sure the way you are was a ploy to keep me interested—one minute hot, one minute cold—the notion of give a wolf a taste and keep him hungry, *n'est-ce pas*? But you, you are not like that. This, at least, *this* I do know.'

'You don't know anything about me, Jacques. Not really,' Holly said painfully, aware as she said the words that he would be quite within his rights to blame her for that. He had told her so much about himself—his childhood, his early years as an adult, his hopes and fears and aspirations. He had been generous with his thoughts and emotions, he had shared most, maybe all, of what he was with her, and she had given him very little in return.

But he didn't accuse her. And when he spoke she realised he had not actually shared all of himself because she'd had no idea he was thinking along the lines his words revealed. 'I know enough to be sure I want you for my wife,' he said huskily. 'Whatever this man was to you, whatever happened, I am sure of this. I want to take care of you as he obviously did not—cherish you, adore you.

Why do you think I have not taken you to my bed before this? Why? Because I want to *marry* you, not have an affair or an open-ended modern relationship. I have had enough of those. I *love* you, Holly. Do you not understand this? And for my wife, for the mother of my children, I have waited. Waited until you trust me, until you allow yourself to take me into your heart and your head as well as your body. *Zut!*'

The oath was harsh, an explosion, and he breathed deeply for a moment before he gained control again. 'So many times I have been tempted to make you mine, and I could have done. Oh, yes, I could have done,' he said grimly. 'We both know this. Even today I made myself a promise that you would be in my bed tonight, that the waiting was over. But a relationship that is destined to go on for a lifetime should begin with absolute truth and trust.'

She stared at him, frozen outwardly but with her mind racing in despair. Until this very moment she would have sworn on oath that should Jacques ever say what he had just said she would fall on his neck in hysterical happiness. *Because she had known it could never happen.* She had been safe in lying to herself. Jacques liked bright, beautiful, successful women he could have a good time with—everyone knew that. Light-hearted flings, brief intrigues, passionate affairs that already had the stopwatch ticking the moment they began—that was Jacques's style. Nothing heavy, nothing serious.

But she believed him absolutely now. The seduction game was one thing but he wasn't playing games with her.

'I have often wondered if I would ever say those words to anyone,' he said after a long moment had gone by. 'I did not think they would look as you do if it happened.'

'I…I'm sorry.' What could she say? How on earth could she make him understand? It wasn't him who was at fault here, but she knew he was a man who, once having committed, would expect everything in return. And when it came—from her—it wouldn't be enough. *She couldn't be what he wanted, what he thought she was.* She could never fulfil his expectations. She didn't know how. And when he discovered that… 'I'm sorry,' she said again, her voice shaking.

'You do not feel the same.'

Feel the same? She adored him, she loved him with every morsel of her being, but how would she ever survive him leaving her if she gave herself to him? She was on first-name terms with rejection and exclusion, but this was something different. When Jacques left she wouldn't be able to go on.

She didn't know her eyes had filled with tears or that her face had mirrored her agony, so when Jacques took her cold little hands in his warm ones it was a surprise. She had expected him to shout at her, to tell her she was— oh, everything she feared he would see in her, she supposed. 'What did he do to you to make you look like that?' he murmured huskily. 'You do not still have feelings for him?'

'No, no.' Oh, the irony of it.

'Holly, you are breaking my heart. I cannot bear to see you like this.'

She was breaking his heart? It shattered the last of her fragile composure, which had taken a battering all night. *Her* heart was beating so hard it was reverberating in her chest, like the worst palpitations imaginable. Her body went rigid, her nerves at breaking point. 'Jacques, this isn't what you think.'

'No?' His voice was tight and very controlled. 'Tell me, *petite*. What am I thinking?'

'I...I can't explain.'

'You cannot or you will not?'

There was such a lump in her throat she didn't know how she managed to push the words over it. 'Can't. Please believe me. Can't.'

'Then where do we go from here? Do you see me as a friend, a benefactor, a business associate, what? Do you see me as a lover, Holly? A ship that passes in the night? Because sure as hell you do not seem to want anything more.'

How did she answer that? There was a quivering silence, but in spite of the fact she knew she was going to lose him she couldn't break it. She had been waiting for this moment since she had acknowledged she loved him, knowing it would come sooner or later. Now it was here she couldn't even begin to think clearly. She didn't understand herself, or how this barbed flirtation with Jacques had escalated into what was now facing her, but the facts were undeniable.

He wanted her to tell all. To open up all the past and the present with its goblins and horrors, and then trust him for the future. And she couldn't. She couldn't. End of story. End of her wonderful job, her dear little apartment, of Paris, the new life. End of Jacques.

Out of the chaos of her thoughts she suddenly made sense of one thing. She had to end this now. She owed him that if nothing else. She had to do what she should have done months ago and disappear.

'I...I resign.'

'*What?*' He was angry now.

'I resign from my job. Does that make it easier?'

'Oh, yes, Holly. That makes it all beautifully easy,' he

said with acid sarcasm. 'I now lose my textile technologist as well as my girlfriend. *C'est extra!*'

'Do you want me to work my notice?' she asked painfully.

'What I *want*…' He stopped abruptly, dark colour flaring under the chiselled cheekbones. 'Oh, to hell with it!'

What he meant was, to hell with *her*, Holly thought painfully.

She raised her head, a measure of bruised pride coming to her rescue as he glared at her, frustration in every line and plane of his body. He muttered something which sounded very rude in his native tongue whilst reaching for her in the same moment, cupping her head tightly in his strong hands and covering her mouth with his.

It was not a gentle or a tender kiss. Every ounce of his bitter disappointment and bafflement was in it, bewildered rage and pain evident as he pulled her against him. There was none of the restraint he had shown thus far; this was a man who had been driven to the very edge of himself and who sensed he was losing something precious.

And she didn't even fight him for one moment. The knowledge was there, hammering at her consciousness, but in seconds she was accepting his kiss hungrily, clutching at him as he levered himself over her.

His hands roamed over her body as his mouth ravished hers, but as she kissed him back with touching abandonment they became lost to the world, drinking in the scent of each other as they touched and tasted.

She couldn't let herself be taken over like this. The old fear rose but his caresses were evoking such sensual stirrings and delight that the fear evaporated, her body ignoring her mind's warning. A restless urgency was tuning her in to his every touch and sigh and all she knew was that she wanted him. Him, Jacques. No other man could make her feel like this and if she didn't make love with him she would make love with no one.

Her mouth was as hungry as his, her hands feeling the bunched muscles in his back as he crouched over her in the close confines of the car, and then suddenly she became aware of the change in him. He had become very still and he wasn't kissing her any longer.

'Jacques?' It was a whisper, and then, as he moved off her and into his seat again, Holly stared at him and saw his face was stiff and grim. 'What's the matter?'

'This is not the way it should be. Not for us. Not for you.' He made a sound low in his throat. 'I do not want to have this kind of an affair with you, damn it! I want to *marry* you and that is different. I want to wake up every morning and know you will be the first thing I see, and when I get home at night I want to know you will be there too. You understand? I want us to make a *life* together; is that so wrong? If we make love tonight I will still only have your body and not your heart, and it is not enough, Holly. It is not enough.'

'You wanted us to be lovers at the beginning,' she said, struggling to control the tears. 'So what has changed?'

'Me.' His voice was hollow. 'Is that not the greatest joke? It is I who have changed, *petite*. I love you and I will be damned if I will take you like this. I want you so badly it is driving me crazy, but I want more than this.'

'You want too much,' she said dully.

'Maybe.' He looked at her, his eyes narrowed and the amber light subdued and murky in the darkness. 'But that is Jacques Querruel, *chérie*. I can be no other way. I have never settled for less than exactly what I want.'

'An all-or-nothing guy?' she whispered painfully, closing her eyes to shut out his face as she lay back in her seat.

'If you like.'

'And if it turns out to be nothing?'

'I have never considered that an option and I do not intend to start now.' He turned the key in the ignition as he spoke, and as the car purred into action Holly averted her face so he would not see the tears spilling down her cheeks in a hot, salty flood.

CHAPTER EIGHT

'YOU aren't seriously telling me you walked out of that dream of a job, not to mention his life, and flew home without a word? That's just not *you*, Holly.'

No, it wasn't, but then she wasn't very sure exactly who she was any more, Holly thought wearily as she surveyed Lucy Holden over a steaming mug of coffee at Lucy's kitchen table.

'I wrote a letter explaining I couldn't stay,' she said flatly after a second or two had slipped by and it was clear Lucy was waiting for a response. 'And I enclosed the keys of the apartment and everything.'

'And that makes it all right? What about when you need a reference for another job?' Lucy bent down and whisked Melanie Anne onto her knee just in time to prevent her angelic-looking daughter from grabbing the cat's tail. The cat, realising its narrow escape, leapt onto Holly's lap, where it began to purr loudly after casting a superior glance at the wriggling baby who was now bellowing in frustration at being thwarted.

'I shan't ask Jacques for one,' Holly said definitely. 'In fact I shan't contact him again at all. It's best to make a clean break. Less painful for both of us.'

'Holly, I'm your friend.' Lucy surveyed her severely from bright blue eyes under a mop of blonde curls. 'And I'd just make the point you look the worst I've ever seen you in my whole life, and that includes the three weeks you spent with us when you looked as if you were at death's door.'

'Thanks.'

'I mean it. This guy, by your own admission, is offering marriage, and don't forget we're talking marriage to a millionaire here. That's got to be a bonus in anyone's book! And you've already said you care about him, so—' Lucy paused, thrusting a chocolate biscuit into Melanie Anne's podgy hand whereupon it was aimed immediately at the cat '—so I just don't see what the problem is here.'

Holly's stomach turned over but she had been expecting this. From the moment she had stepped foot in the apartment last night she'd known what she had to do. She had telephoned the airport and obtained an early-morning flight and then spent the next few hours packing and cleaning the apartment. After writing a letter to Jacques she had telephoned for a taxi at the unearthly hour of five in the morning, and had left the building in the pink haze of dawn.

After she had made the decision to remain in Paris when Jacques offered her the post permanently, she had notified the landlord that she no longer required her bedsit and had told him to pass on all her bed linen and towels and other incidentals to Mrs Gibson. It had been a furnished let so there had been no problem about storing furniture or anything like that, and Holly had already deposited a large box of miscellaneous personal items with Mrs Gibson when she'd first left for France, thinking that if the job did work out she could pick them up some time in the future.

And so she had arrived in England homeless but knowing there would be a welcome and a bed for her with James and Lucy. She had also known that if she threw herself on her old friends for sanctuary they deserved a full explanation, which would not be easy. She had never told anyone about David's attack and just how badly the social services had got it wrong.

She stared at Lucy now, and something in her face made Lucy say, 'What? What is it?' before adding, 'Look, I'm going to put Melanie Anne down for her nap and then we can talk properly. OK?'

'OK.' She wasn't looking forward to this but it had to be.

An hour and a box of tissues later the two women sat looking at each other after what had been an emotionally fraught sixty minutes for both of them. They had cried together and hugged a lot, which had been therapeutic for Holly, and now Lucy was saying, 'We always knew there was something more than you had told us. Oh, Holly, what a rotten time of it you had. I would kill anyone who tried to lay a finger on Melanie Anne.'

Holly smiled weakly at the vehemence in Lucy's voice. 'And I'd be right behind you in case you didn't finish the job.'

'I suppose it's no use my saying that you're fantastic and beautiful and a lovely person, and that all your fears regarding Jacques falling out of love with you are nonsense?' Lucy asked softly. 'That it's got every chance of being a forever story?'

Holly shook her head. 'I just can't be what he would want,' she said slowly. 'I know it, in here.' She touched her chest. 'I'd destroy us both with my insecurities and lack of trust in him, however patient he might try to be. And if he stayed with me out of pity...' She shook her head despairingly.

'Aren't you rather jumping the gun here?' Lucy said practically. 'You're assuming the absolute worst. What if you marry him and he's everything you want and you're everything he wants? It does happen, you know. Look at me and James.'

Wordlessly Holly shook her head again.

'Holly, you're brave and strong, so much stronger than you realise,' Lucy said passionately. 'And you say you love him with all your heart. Please, please don't throw this chance away. Just because the poor guy is loaded as well as handsome you can't hold that against him. And don't forget ordinary Mr Joe Bloggs is capable of infidelity as well as someone like Jacques.'

'Is that supposed to make me feel better?' Holly asked with a watery smile. And then, as Lucy went to say more, she held up her hand. 'Lucy, I know where you are coming from and I appreciate you and James more than words can say, but please, I've made up my mind about this. Can…can we talk about something else now?'

Lucy wriggled in her seat. 'Oh, *Holly*.'

'Please? And will you make me a promise that you or James won't try to contact Jacques or let him know where I am?'

'Of course we wouldn't.' Lucy looked horrified. 'I think you're crazy, and I wish you would change your mind, but I wouldn't dream of betraying your trust like that, neither would James.'

'Thank you.' Holly reached across the table and placed her hand on Lucy's arm for a moment. 'And you don't mind if I stay for a while till I find a job and a place to live? I'll pay board, of course—my bank balance is extremely healthy after the last few months—but I'd rather be with you and James than in a hotel or something.'

'I should think you would!' Lucy took a sip of coffee—their third pot since Holly had knocked on the front door two hours earlier—before saying, 'Stay as long as you want; you know we'd love to have you, and the guest-room bed is already made up.'

James expressed exactly the same sentiments when he arrived home later that evening, even before Lucy told him about Jacques and her hasty flight from France. Lucy waited until she and her husband were alone before she mentioned David Kirby, but the next morning James let Holly know he had the full picture in typical James fashion by giving her a big hug and stating grimly that some men ought to be castrated, before leaving for the university.

Holly watched him go fondly. She loved this couple and little Melanie Anne, and if she hadn't been feeling so utterly wretched she would have thoroughly enjoyed staying with them.

It was during the time Holly tackled the huge mound of ironing Lucy admitted had been growing for a couple of weeks—'I *loathe* ironing and I always put it off and put if off until it's mountainous, which then makes it worse!'—that she decided she was going to take a year or two off career-wise.

She'd get something completely different—waitressing maybe, or perhaps bar work or even working in a shop. She needed to chill out mentally and she couldn't face working in another office for ages. She didn't admit to herself here that if she tried for the sort of position she had trained for there was just the slightest possibility Jacques might be able to trace her, and Lucy made no comment when Holly told her what she had decided beyond raising quizzical eyebrows.

James and Lucy had left their apartment and moved to a small three-bedroomed terraced house in Wimbledon once Lucy's pregnancy was confirmed, but, even though James's job paid well and Lucy worked part-time at a local private hospital two days a week when Melanie Anne was at nursery, money was a little tight with Christmas approaching, Lucy confided once the ironing was done. How about if Holly left looking for somewhere to stay until after the New Year? That way they had a temporary lodger, which would help household finances enormously, Melanie Anne could get to know her Aunty Holly properly, and Holly wouldn't be all alone in a new bedsit for Christmas.

Holly rather suspected it was the last reason which was more on Lucy's mind than anything else, but in truth she had been dreading being by herself so soon after leaving Jacques. He was in every thought, filling her mind when she was awake and invading her dreams, and she had cried for hours the night before. She was glad she had told someone about David at last—in a way it had been a huge relief—but raking it all up again had been like salt on a raw wound. A few weeks with Lucy and James would be balm on her bruised and bleeding emotions. And so she had accepted Lucy's offer thankfully.

Two days later Holly secured a job in a local café that also doubled as a baker's and had its own shop. The hours were long and the work was tiring, and the staff had to be prepared to be jacks of all trades, but it paid well. The owners—a husband-and-wife team—were kindly employers who worked as hard as their employees, and the two other girls were pleasant and good-natured.

Holly knew she was lucky to have found such a position so quickly, and Lucy and James went out of their way to make her feel wanted and loved, but, nevertheless, she was so unhappy she felt as if she was living in a dark vacuum most of the time. Useless to tell herself things would get better, that she would adapt, that everything had turned out for the best—she seemed to miss Jacques more and not less as the days and weeks crawled by. But never, at any time, did she doubt she had done the right thing. Which was scant comfort in the circumstances.

Jacques would meet someone else, someone fresh and bright and beautiful, someone with no skeletons in the cupboard and without enough baggage to fill a ten-ton skip.

The week before Christmas Holly went to see Mrs Gibson and Mr Bateman, loaded down with presents for them and—of course—Mrs Gibson's cats. She spent a cosy Sunday afternoon with them in Mrs Gibson's bedsit, drinking tea and eating homemade coconut cake, and told them far more than she had intended to do about Jacques, due mainly to Mrs Gibson's persistent questioning.

Mrs Gibson, her bright orange hair toning perfectly with the big ginger tomcat draped in purring ecstasy round her bony shoulders like a green-eyed stole, thought it all wonderfully tragic and romantic, especially when Holly made them both promise to keep her whereabouts a secret should anyone enquire.

And at eleven o'clock the next morning Holly glanced up from the box of cream cakes she had just packaged for a customer and saw Jacques standing in front of her. The box fell unheeded to the floor and her hand went to her throat, and one of the other girls—who obviously thought she was about to faint—grabbed at her arm as she yelled for assistance.

'I...I'm all right,' she whispered, her gaze still locked with the amber eyes she remembered so well, the eyes that had featured in all her dreams for weeks. He was standing no more than six feet away, not moving, not talking, just looking at her. She blinked and then rubbed her eyes, but he was still there. How had he found her?

She wasn't aware she had spoken the words out loud,

but when he answered, saying quietly, 'Mrs Gibson telephoned me after you left yesterday. I've got to know her
quite well since you've been gone,' she was dumbstruck.

She was aware she was shaking uncontrollably and also
that Alice, at the side of her, was hugely interested in the
proceedings, but for the life of her she couldn't move or
speak.

He looked wonderful. Magnificent. But thinner, much
thinner, and older. She felt a rush of love surge through
her that was so almighty her head swam with it. Oh, my
love, my love. Why have you come? Why couldn't you
have let it be? And she forced herself to say, 'Please go,
Jacques.'

'Not on your life,' he answered steadily. 'Get your coat;
we have some talking to do.'

'I...I can't just leave; this is my job.'

He didn't point out that was exactly what she had done
before, which in the circumstances he thought showed
great restraint. He merely repeated very quietly, 'Get your
coat, Holly.'

'Do you want me to call Mr Bishop?' Alice was all
agog.

'Call whoever you like,' Jacques said pleasantly, still
with his eyes on Holly's white face.

'No, no.' This was turning into a farce. 'Tell...tell them
I've taken an early lunch break,' Holly said weakly to
Alice.

'Tell them they need a new assistant.'

'*Jacques.*'

'Yes, my sweet?'

Holly decided to get her coat. He was waiting by the
door when she emerged from the private quarters of the
business, arms folded across his chest and big body relaxed. Only he wasn't. She knew him well enough now

to know that the lazy pose was a sham. And Mrs Bishop was standing by the side of him, having returned from a visit to the bank. The pair had obviously been talking because Mrs Bishop said, somewhat dazedly, 'We shan't expect you in again today, Holly,' before giving Jacques a wide, warm smile.

How did he do that? Holly asked herself helplessly. He had obviously charmed the pants off the normally astute and very down-to-earth woman because Monday afternoons were always hectic, and Mrs Bishop wasn't usually so charitable in dispensing time off at the drop of a hat.

She had expected him to start the inquest as soon as they were outside, but he merely took her arm and walked her along the busy pavement. The shops were full of Christmas lights and decorations and the air was cold and sharp. Despite herself Holly felt heady with bitter-sweet joy at seeing him again, even though her heart was jerking in wild, panicked beats. He seemed very large and dark at the side of her, the big charcoal overcoat he was wearing increasing the impression of controlled masculinity. She nerved herself and glanced at him through her eyelashes. He had definitely lost some weight, she thought dizzily. It made him look even more ruthless, and sexier...

'Where are we going?' She forced the words out through the whirlwind in her head.

He didn't look at her, his voice cool and determined as he said shortly, 'Somewhere we can talk.'

'You shouldn't have come here.'

He pulled her into him slightly, shielding her with his body from contact with a group of noisy teenagers who were taking up most of the pavement. 'Yes, I should,' he said grimly.

They reached a long, sleek car that Holly rather suspected was a Ferrari parked expertly in between two family saloons at the side of the road. 'Get in.' Jacques had opened the door for her and she had no option but to slide into the leather-clad interior, her heart still thudding. She couldn't quite work out where he was coming from. He had every right to be furiously angry, but if he was he was controlling it well. But then he would, she reminded herself miserably. Control was Jacques's middle name.

'You're too slender.'

They had been driving for five minutes when Jacques spoke and Holly's heart kicked against her ribs.

'More beautiful than ever but too slender,' he said huskily. 'Haven't you been eating properly?'

'Have you?' she countered weakly.

'No, but then I wasn't the one who left.' Amber eyes flashed their golden light across her pale face.

'That doesn't mean...' She stopped abruptly.

'Yes?' he prompted softly.

'Just because I was the one who left doesn't mean I didn't care,' she managed faintly.

'You just did not care enough?' It was a rapier thrust straight for the heart and Holly reflected painfully that he hadn't lost his touch.

What could she say? She glanced at him again but the hard profile was looking straight ahead at the heavy lunchtime traffic now. 'It...it wasn't like that.'

'Maybe, maybe not, but I intend to find out exactly what is what before too much longer,' he said grimly. 'So accept that now and it will make things a hell of a lot easier for us both.'

Holly took a deep breath and prayed for a revelation on how to handle this. Nothing came. This time he wasn't going to be fobbed off and there was nowhere left to run. His face told her that. He was determined to find out why a relationship—a marriage—between them was impossible. Why she would fail him and in failing him destroy everything between them. Why she couldn't *trust* him. Because that was what all this came down to in the end. If she loved him so much, and she did, and she couldn't trust that he would continue to love her, that in itself would destroy his love.

She bit hard on her lip, her head feeling as though it would burst. One of her less sympathetic foster mothers had called her a nutcase once, and somehow—in spite of much worse insults from her peers at times—that had stuck with her, maybe because it had come from an adult. But perhaps Meg Connor had been right. Who else but a crazy woman would refuse Jacques Querruel?

'Eat first or talk first?'

'What?' She came out of the bitter maelstrom of her thoughts at the sound of his voice, and then said shakily, 'Talk.' Time had run out. She would tell him it all and then he would have to accept there couldn't be a future for them. Perhaps he wouldn't even want there to be after she had revealed the person she really was, deep inside. He could have anyone he wanted. Why would he bother with her?

'Good.'

He said nothing after the one cryptic word until they got to the open expanse of Richmond Park. Delicately proportioned, gentle-eyed deer were wandering under the trees in the far distance, and as he parked the car Holly thought how ironic it was that the final death blow to their future should occur in such beautiful surroundings. The blue winter sky overhead, the bare trees with their stark and majestic silhouettes and the red of the animals below added a poignancy to it all that made her want to howl.

Instead she steeled herself and turned to him, determined her control would match his. 'This wasn't a good idea, Jacques. It would have been far better to leave things as they were.'

'Really?' he replied, pinning her with that clear golden gaze that seemed to pierce straight into her soul. 'I disagree. But then perhaps some men would enjoy searching fruitlessly for weeks on end for someone who walked out on them without a word. Maybe they would get something out of doing the rounds of people they thought might be able to help them, of employing private detectives, of visiting eccentric old ladies every week in the hope that the object of their search might have made contact. Although, on reflection, Mrs Gibson was perhaps the only bright spot in a succession of long, dreary days. Because that's how things were, Holly. That's how I've been spending my time since you vanished.'

'I didn't expect you to do that,' she said in a tight voice. *Private detectives?* He had hired private detectives?

'Obviously not.' It was very dry.

His remoteness enabled her to inject a little attitude into her voice as she said, 'And what did you promise Mrs Gibson to make her rat on me anyway?'

'Rat on you?' He turned to face her, one arm on the steering wheel. 'Holly, I am not a gangster and Mrs Gibson is not a—what is the word?—stool pigeon.'

'That's two words.'

'She's neither.' He lifted her chin with determined fingers. 'Look at me, Holly, and listen. I want answers. I do not care if we sit here all day but I will have them. I have never pursued a woman like I have you, I have never trodden on eggshells for a woman like I have you, and I have certainly never waited for a woman like I have you. But enough is enough. You understand?'

He paused, moving his hands to cup her white face. 'I love you,' he said quietly, 'and I am going to kiss you.

Then I am going to ask you some questions and you will answer them.'

The kiss was a long one and at the end of it Holly knew her trembling would have communicated itself to him, pressed as she was against his hardness. He released her slowly, reluctantly, and then he said, 'Holly, who is David Kirby and what place did he have in your life, and that of Christina? And before you answer me I will tell you that I have made it my business to go and see Christina.'

She stared at him, wide-eyed and as white as a sheet.

'And she would tell me nothing,' he continued softly. 'Nothing at all. Neither would her husband. But I know this man hurt you both in some way and I want to know the truth. He is a spectre between us and I will not have that.'

She shut her eyes to block out his face. 'David Kirby was not a boyfriend or lover, as you imagined,' she said woodenly. 'I...I have never had a boyfriend...before you.'

His hands were still either side of her face and his warmth was soaking into her, making her realise how cold she was. But this was a coldness from deep within and nothing to do with externals.

Jacques did not move or speak for a moment and then he said, very gently, 'You still have not answered my question, *petite*.'

'I told you I was fostered from when I was a little baby, that I was with several families until I was old enough to look after myself? Well, that's true, but for the first eight years I was with a couple I looked upon as my parents. Oh, I knew they weren't, of course, biologically, but they were wonderful people. Then they got sick. I was sent to another home. David and Cassie Kirby's home. They were wealthy, good-looking, charismatic. Christina was fostered by them too, and a young boy named John.'

She jerked her head free now, opening her eyes and turning away from him to look blindly out of the window. 'So there were three of us in all and they showered us with toys and presents. Everyone thought I was lucky to be put with them. But I knew something was wrong, right from the beginning almost I sensed...'

She swallowed painfully, tears running silently down her cheeks. 'He came to my bedroom often. At first he just wanted me to sit on his knee. He'd read to me, things like that, and hug and kiss me goodnight, but...not as you should a child. Then one day when I'd been there a few months, when he thought I was under his control like Christina and the other child, he—' she took a hard pull of air '—he tried to rape me.'

She felt him jerk and then he took her into his arms. She didn't resist but neither did she look at him, burying her face in his chest. 'I fought him and eventually he gave up, but he told lies about me. He made Christina lie too. I was put with another family but I was scared and confused... Everything went wrong from then on.'

She could feel the slam of his heart against his ribcage and the rigid control he was keeping of himself, but she still didn't dare look at him. Her heart was thundering in her ears and she was terrified of what she would read in his face if she looked at him. Because she mustn't weaken in what she had to do.

And then his voice came, a low, rumbling growl. 'This man, this David Kirby. Where is he now?'

'Dead,' she whispered, rubbing at her eyes with her hand but keeping her head on his chest. 'There was going to be a court case, something to do with children at a youth club he helped out with. Christina came forward then and he…he killed himself.'

'Pity.' It was grim. 'I would have liked to meet him and do the job myself.' There was a pause and then he said, 'How old were you when that happened? When he killed himself?'

'I was at university.'

'So all that time you had been coping with this alone? Was it the reason you were moved from family to family?' he asked gently.

She nodded against his bulk. 'I was a problem child,' she said in a small voice.

He stroked his hand over the ruffled silk of her hair and then along her damp cheek. 'Look at me, *chérie*,' he said softly. And when she shook her head, he said tenderly, 'You were never a problem, this I know. Brave and plucky for sure, and strong and courageous, but this can be seen as defiance by the insensitive and ignorant.'

'Don't.' It was in the form of a small wail.

'Don't what?'

'I can't…' She raised her head now, her throat tight with the emotion she was battling to control. 'I can never be what you want me to be, Jacques. What you need. You must see that now?'

'What I see is a beautiful, fine woman.'

'Jacques, I can't live up to what you would expect of me. What you would have a right to expect of a wife. I told you, I haven't even had a boyfriend before, let alone a lover.'

'Because you were waiting for me,' he said softly. 'I told you before, *chérie*, it was fate who pointed us out to each other, and do not try to tell me that things would not be good between us in bed because I know different. I have held you, touched and tasted you. Trust me on this.'

'But that's just it.' She strained away from him. 'That's what I can't do.' He still didn't understand.

'Holly, I do not expect some sort of performance in bed,' he said patiently. 'Surely you understand this? Do you think I had not realised that you are not very experienced?'

'I don't mean about the physical side of our relationship,' she said miserably. 'At least, not just that. I don't know how to explain this.'

'Try,' he said wryly, 'before I go mad.'

'It wouldn't be so bad if I didn't love you, but I do, and…and if we did marry I'd be wondering all the time when you were going to tire of me. I've seen the way women throw themselves at you and sooner or later someone would come along… It wouldn't really even be your fault,' she finished weakly.

'Oh, thank you,' he said flatly. 'Not only am I a Don Juan who can't keep his hands off women and who would commit adultery at the drop of a hat, but now I am weak and spineless too?'

'I didn't say that.' It was coming out all wrong.

'That is exactly what you said, Holly. What do you expect me to do? I have made a great deal of money, I admit it, but through hard work and my own efforts. I do not intend to apologise for that. Neither can I help my physical appearance. You must take my parents to task for that. But my mind and my principles are my own and I happen to believe in fidelity within marriage.'

'But even if you didn't actually…do anything you would want to,' she said desperately. 'I'm not the one for you, don't you see? Your world is so different from mine—'

'Holly.' His voice was too loud and she watched him take a long pull of air before he said more quietly,

'*Chérie*, I can understand how what has happened has made you insecure and vulnerable—'

'No, it's not that,' she said thickly. 'You're not an ordinary man, Jacques, you're not, and I am very ordinary. It just wouldn't work. A brief affair maybe, but not marriage.'

'You are wrong, Holly,' he said quietly. 'So wrong. I am just as assailable as the next man, for a start, but you are an extraordinary woman. Quite extraordinary. And I do not want an affair with you, brief or otherwise. I want to marry you. To live with you as husband and wife. You have to believe me on this.' His voice was low but very intense.

Her stomach turned over. 'I can't,' she whispered, and soft though the words were Jacques recognised the finality in them.

He stared at her for a moment, his face darkening, and Holly knew he was trying to keep a hold on his temper. He looked angry; she had never seen him so angry. 'And I have no say in this?' he bit out grimly. 'Is that it? You are allowed to destroy both our lives and I am supposed to accept it? Well, I do not! I do not, do you hear? I am not going to apologise for being who I am and I cannot control whether other women find me attractive, damn it! But since I met you I do not even notice other females, and that's the truth. I only want you, now and always. I love you, Holly, and I want to marry you. I shall always love you. What the hell more can I say?'

'Nothing,' she said, her mouth trembling. 'It's not you, it's me. I know that.'

'Well, bully for you,' he said bitterly, his French accent all the more prevalent with the English-sounding phrase. 'What if I had been poor and ugly, what then? Would you have married me then?'

'Don't...don't be like this.'

'That should be my line in the circumstances, don't you think?' he said furiously. 'Holly, I'll give you all the time you need, reassure you every day for the rest of our lives if that is what it takes, but you cannot shut me out of your life and your heart. I'm in there now and I mean to stay. Your problems are my problems now; we'll deal with them together. It is not just you any more, don't you understand? What affects you affects me. You are looking on this as though we are two people and separate, but I do not see it that way. We are not talking about you or me—marriage is an us. We become one. You draw on my strengths and I draw on yours. I help you with your demons and you help me with mine.'

It sounded fine, in theory. 'You have no demons,' she said quietly, her head lifting in defiance. 'You know it. Yours were conquered years ago.'

'Every man, woman and child has things they need help with. I am not an island any more than you are. And that is how you have tried to live since you were eight, *n'est-ce pas*? But you cannot go on like this. Kirby is the past and he should be dead and buried in your mind as well as physically. If not he is still hurting you and you cannot live all your life with his sickness touching you.'

The concept shocked her and she looked at him as resentment and rage rose inside her. 'How dare you say that?' she said furiously. 'He has no hold over me, none at all.'

'Prove it.' The amber eyes were very dark, like burnt honey. 'Say you are prepared to take a chance on loving me, on being my wife. Say you will trust me if you cannot trust yourself. I love you with all my being, all my soul. You hold my heart in your hands. Marry me, Holly.'

There was a long silence and Holly couldn't speak. She

was aware that she was crying soundlessly, the tears streaming down her face, but he made no move to hold her or caress her and she knew why. This was decision time. A man like Jacques wouldn't keep asking; he had too much pride for that. He had bared his soul in a manner that was completely alien to him and he had given her all he could. But it wasn't enough. For right or wrong, it wasn't enough.

'No.'

There was another silence, which seemed endless, and then Jacques turned the key in the ignition and the engine growled into life.

It was over.

CHAPTER NINE

'NEW YEAR'S EVE. It doesn't seem like New Year's Eve somehow, does it?' Alice stretched bony arms and then tweaked down her bright red miniskirt, which had ridden up over her thick black tights. 'You doing anything special, Holly?'

'No.' Holly forced a smile. 'Unless you call babysitting my godchild special. Lucy and James have been invited to a neighbour's party so I said I'd stay with Melanie Anne. They protested but I wasn't going to go out anyway.'

Alice nodded but Holly could tell she wasn't on the other girl's wavelength. At nineteen years of age, Alice was still of the opinion that 'night' was spelt 'nightclubs' and the ultimate tragedy was staying in on a night when everyone else was partying.

'A group of us are going to Trafalgar Square.' Alice giggled, flicking back her Gothic black bob. 'You might see us on the news tomorrow night. You know, drunk and disorderly and all that jazz!'

'I look forward to it,' Holly said wryly, before another batch of customers claimed their attention and effectively finished all chance of conversation for the last few minutes the shop was open.

The bakery-cum-café was just a short walk away from James and Lucy's house, and as always during the ten minutes it took to reach their home Holly's thoughts focused on Jacques. It had been two weeks since she had seen him that last time and she'd ached for him every

172

moment. The deep well of loneliness which had always been a part of her since she had left her first foster parents, Kate and Angus, had grown over the last days. She had hoped it would get better but instead it had got worse.

Christmas had been a nightmare, the worst part being that she had felt forced to put on a show of being heart-whole and cheerful for Lucy and James, and not least little Melanie Anne. And all the time the last conversation with Jacques had been going round and round in her head, beating at her brain until she had felt it would explode.

He had dropped her off outside her place of work that lunchtime without saying another word until she was on the pavement, where he'd joined her. Then he had taken her hand, his voice controlled and his face grim as he'd said, 'You can't shut me out of your heart and your head, Holly. Don't you know that yet? It's too late. Way, way too late.'

And then he had turned and left her and driven away in his expensive sports car. And she hadn't heard from him again.

All over Christmas she had been waiting for a call, even a visit, but there had been nothing. *Nothing.* Which was what she had wanted... Only it wasn't. But then the thought of making the sort of commitment he was asking for terrified her. How could she love Jacques as fully and unreservedly as he would expect, as he *deserved*, when she felt chained by so many fears and doubts? She couldn't, she told herself frequently. But then how could she live without him in her life now she knew him? She couldn't. And so it went on.

Every day since Christmas she had expected, with every tinkle of the bakery doorbell, to see Jacques standing there in front of her when she glanced up. But it hadn't happened. *He* hadn't happened. He had taken her at her word and disappeared out of her life, and she didn't know how she was going to bear it.

Tears misted the road in front of her and she blinked them away quickly. No self-pity, she told herself savagely. She had had her chance with Jacques and she'd blown it, and if she was being truthful she couldn't in all honesty say she wouldn't do the same again. Nothing had changed, not really. Nothing, it seemed, except Jacques's feelings for her, which it appeared he could put on and take off at will. And, that being the case, it proved her absolutely right, didn't it? But then she had known someone as proud and strong as Jacques wouldn't keep banging his head against the proverbial brick wall.

'Right, pull-yourself-together time.' As Lucy and James's house came into view Holly sniffed loudly and blinked furiously. Time to be happy-clappy again.

Circles of muted gold from the street lights were casting their soft glow on the pavement as she walked the last few yards, and there was already the nip of frost in the biting air. She had used to love nights like this, especially when there was the faint fragrance of woodsmoke in the air from a neighbouring bonfire like tonight, but now the clean, sharp night didn't move her. Would she ever feel remotely at peace again? She stood at the entrance to the three feet or so of paved front garden and lifted her face to the sky. It was pierced with stars and eternally beautiful.

'Holly? Is that you?'

The front door opening suddenly and Lucy's voice nearly made her jump out of her skin, and her heart was beating like a drum when she said, 'Of course it's me. What's the matter?'

'Oh, Holly. Quick, come in.'

There was a note in Lucy's voice which made Holly

fairly spring up the couple of steps to the hall, and then she stopped dead at the sight of Mrs Gibson standing in the doorway to Lucy's sitting room. Holly hadn't seen her old neighbour since Jacques's disastrous visit. She didn't bear the old lady any animosity—Mrs Gibson would have thought she was doing the best thing in telling Jacques where she lived and worked, Holly knew that, or else wild horses wouldn't have dragged the information from her. But she just hadn't felt like seeing anyone.

'What is it, Mrs Gibson?' It was clear the old lady was distressed, and normally she didn't budge more than a few yards from her home and cats. 'Is Mr Bateman all right?'

'Mr Bateman?' Mrs Gibson's scathing and expressive snort suggested extreme scorn. 'That man managed to put the dustbin lid down when Tigger was inside a few days ago. I had people combing the streets for him when he didn't come back for two days; he's lucky to be alive. How he didn't suffocate I don't know. And of course it would be the one time Mr Bateman remembered to weight the lid down with bricks. He was hungry and upset and he smelt to high heaven.'

Holly assumed Mrs Gibson was referring to Tigger in the last sentence. 'Oh, dear.' She shook her head sympathetically. 'Then why are you here?'

'Why am I…? Oh, yes, yes. How silly of me. That's Mr Bateman distracting me,' Mrs Gibson said, quite unfairly. 'It's that nice young man, Jacques, I've called about.'

Here we go. It was clear Mrs Gibson saw herself as the New Year goodwill fairy with a matchmaking hat on, Holly thought darkly, drawing on every ounce of patience as she said quietly, 'I'd prefer not to discuss Jacques Querruel, Mrs Gibson. We were seeing each other for a time but it is over. End of story.'

'Really?' Mrs Gibson nodded. And then, as Lucy went to speak, the old lady waved her to silence, before saying, 'I'm surprised at that. I know he thought a bit of you. ''Milly,'' he said—did you know he called me Milly?' she asked Holly abruptly.

'Er—no, no, I didn't.'

'Oh, yes. The first afternoon he came to tea with me—when he was still searching all the hours of the day and night for you—we decided on Jacques and Milly. It's short for Millicent, of course.'

'Right.' Holly struggled to keep her voice in neutral. Mrs Gibson's tone had made it quite clear how she viewed the current situation and whose side she was on, and it wasn't Holly's. As far as Holly was aware, no one had ever had the temerity to address the fierce old lady by her Christian name—probably including the late Mr Gibson—but of course it had only taken Jacques an hour or two to charm Mrs Gibson into fluttering submission!

'Now, where was I?' Mrs Gibson glared at Holly and Lucy as though they had been the means of distracting her. 'Oh, yes, that's right. I was telling you what the dear boy said to me.'

'Mrs Gibson—'

'''Milly,'' he said—' Mrs Gibson completely ignored Holly's attempt to interrupt her '''—I know I have met the woman I want to spend the rest of my life with, and whatever it takes I shall find her again.'' What do you say to that, then?' she asked Holly confrontationally.

'Like I said, Mrs Gibson, it's over,' Holly said firmly.

'Lucy said you would say that.'

'And she was right.' And the fact that Jacques hadn't contacted her in any way since their last meeting seemed to suggest he'd got over her pretty quick too! Holly knew the thought which had tormented her day and night was probably totally unjust as far as Jacques was concerned, but it seemed as if a procession of beautiful, available females paraded themselves before her wherever she looked these days. On the TV, in advertisements, books, magazines—gorgeous, fancy-free lovelies who would be perfect for a young and handsome millionaire.

'So you wouldn't be interested in knowing about the dear boy's dreadful accident, then? Out of sight, out of mind, is it?' Mrs Gibson's bright, bird-like eyes were fixed hard on Holly's face.

'What…what did you say?' Holly's heart slammed against her ribcage with enough force to choke her breath.

'It happened early on Christmas Eve morning, of all days, apparently,' Mrs Gibson went on relentlessly. 'A collision with a car that had swerved onto the wrong side of the road to avoid a child who had run out in front of it. And of course these motorbikes don't give the sort of protection a car affords, do they? Mr Gibson drove one as a young man but I soon put a stop to that when I met him.'

'You're saying Jacques's hurt? He's not…?'

'Dead? Oh, dear me, no. Did I give you that impression?' Mrs Gibson asked without a trace of apology in her voice. Short, sharp shock treatment. That was what she'd decided on when she had finished talking with Jacques's housekeeper. This ridiculous situation had gone on long enough and Holly needed bringing to her senses. 'I understand he was unconscious for a good few days, which caused a great deal of anxiety for his family, but there, I mustn't bother you any more. You must be wanting your tea. I'll just get my hat and coat—'

'Please, Mrs Gibson…'

Mrs Gibson took pity on the young, white-faced woman in front of her then, her manner softening as she said quietly, 'I don't know a great deal more than what I have told you, Holly, except that I understand he is out of immediate danger. I only telephoned the number he had given me this morning, you see. I hadn't heard from him, which I thought was a little strange, considering he had promised to call by over Christmas.'

'He had?'

'Oh, yes. He was intending to spend the holiday in England.' Mrs Gibson stared at her meaningfully. 'Where his heart is. His housekeeper said he had only gone a short distance from the château when the accident occurred, however. I think the family would have liked to let you know but they had no way of contacting you, and of course Jacques was in a coma.'

Coma. Oh, God. Please, please, God, don't let him be badly hurt. 'Out of immediate danger'. What did that mean? He could be permanently disabled, anything, and they would still say that. *He could have died.* He could have died and she would never have known but for Mrs Gibson. Please, God, please help me to get to him quickly. Don't let him have a relapse or anything...

By nine o'clock that evening Holly was aboard a plane flying over the Channel.

She had spoken to Monique before she had left, and the housekeeper had immediately burst into tears at the sound of her voice, which had scared Holly to death. She had had the worst thirty seconds of her life, but once Monique had calmed down enough to talk to her it appeared Jacques was no worse and no better than he had been earlier that day when Mrs Gibson had telephoned.

'Severe concussion and two broken legs,' Monique had informed her tearfully when Holly had asked about Jacques's condition. There had been some internal injuries but the doctors seemed satisfied these were no longer a problem. Of course, he was still very ill and at this stage they were just taking it a day at a time. Nothing could be guaranteed...

The plane journey and cab ride to the private hospital on the outskirts of Paris forever remained a blur in Holly's memory. All she could think about was Jacques.

She had done nothing but push him away from the first moment she'd met him. She had rejected him, refused to trust him, failed him so badly she wouldn't have blamed him if he wanted nothing more to do with her after that last caustic meeting in England. *But he had been coming to see her.* Monique had confirmed what Mrs Gibson had intimated. He had set out early on Christmas Eve morning in order to be with her over Christmas. *To be with her.*

How could she have been so stupid? How could she have imagined, for one moment, that she could possibly live without him? If anything happened to him she would die, she would. She wouldn't want to go on living. This was all her fault. If she hadn't sent him away that day he wouldn't have been making the journey that had almost killed him. That still *could* kill him if something went wrong. What if the doctors had missed something? You read about that sort of thing every day in the newspapers. No one was infallible and the best of doctors were only human.

What if she got to the hospital and he had changed his mind about her after everything that had happened? After the accident? What if he now finally believed her when she said she couldn't trust him? She had believed it; she still did in a way. It seemed impossible that a man like Jacques would continue to love her forever and ever, but compared to him being taken permanently by death *now*, in the immediate future, everything else paled into insignificance.

When Holly arrived at the hospital she found to her surprise that she was expected, and as she was whisked along thickly carpeted corridors by a fresh-faced young nurse she blessed Monique, who had obviously telephoned to prepare the way.

Barbe was sitting waiting for her in the corridor outside Jacques's room, and his sister immediately leapt to her feet at the sight of Holly and opened her arms wide, giving her a big hug as she murmured, 'I'm so glad you've come, Holly. We all are. The rest of the family have gone home to sleep—we're all exhausted—but it was decided I remain and meet you.'

'Thank you.' It was more than she deserved. 'How is he?'

'He's got his head back, which is the main thing,' Barbe said with a weak smile. 'It frightened us, seeing Jacques so lifeless and still over the past days. He's always so full of energy, so vital, you know?'

Holly nodded. Yes, she knew.

'He's still sleeping most of the time but at least when he is awake he knows us now. As for his legs...it will take time, the doctors say, but hopefully they will mend, although the right one is very badly damaged. He may always have a limp.'

'Oh, Barbe.' The knot in the pit of her stomach was burning, stifling her breath and choking her. All she wanted now was to see Jacques. To sit with him, to kiss him, to love him. For as long as he wanted her. 'Does...does he know I'm coming?' she whispered thickly.

Barbe looked at her, a straight look, which, although

friendly, said more than any words could have done. She shook her head slowly. 'It seemed best to wait.'

In case she had changed her mind. Holly nodded at the other woman even as her mind told her Jacques's family had no idea of just how much she loved him. Which made them all the more gracious in their acceptance of her arrival at the hospital tonight. 'Can I go in?'

'Of course. I'm going home now, so give Jacques my love.'

The nurse had disappeared at some point, and now it was Jacques's sister who pushed open the door for Holly to enter the dimly lit room beyond, whispering as she did so, 'Monique has got your room ready at the château for when you leave here, OK?'

There were none of the tubes and drips Holly had mentally prepared herself for, just a large cage under the covers, protecting Jacques's damaged legs. She moved quietly forward, her heart accelerating, and then she was by his side of the bed, peering down at the sleeping occupant. It was Jacques and yet not Jacques. He was very still and she didn't think she had ever seen him still before, and very, very pale, almost grey-faced. His black hair fell across his brow in a way he would never have allowed normally, his long eyelashes lying on cheekbones that were starkly chiselled in the whiteness of the skin surrounding them. Holly felt as though her heart was being wrenched out by its roots.

Oh, Jacques, Jacques. Holly swallowed at the constriction in her throat, fighting back the tears which had been gathering behind a great dam since the moment she had seen Mrs Gibson. But she couldn't cry now, not here. He might wake up and she didn't want his first sight of her to be when she was weeping. But she loved him. So, so much. And she desperately wanted to believe they could make it.

She closed her eyes briefly, telling herself she had to be strong for him right now and that the future would work itself out, and when she opened them again Jacques was looking at her.

'Hello, my darling.' It was the first time she had ever used the endearment although she wasn't aware of it until much later. Her mouth began to tremble as he didn't respond in any way at all, simply staring at her with amber eyes that glowed dark gold in the dimly lit and expensively furnished surroundings. She bent down, brushing her lips lightly over his, and then, as she felt his arms come tightly round her, she found herself half lying across his chest as his mouth fastened on hers with a fierceness that belied his condition.

'I...I'll hurt you.' As she came up for air she tried to pull herself off him, only for his arms to tighten still more.

'I can't believe you're real.' It was a low murmur but the deep, sensuous voice was definitely all Jacques's. 'When I saw you standing there I thought I was dreaming again. So many dreams of you...'

He kissed her again, hard and long and not at all as a desperately sick man should kiss. Not that she'd kissed any.

'Jacques, I'm too heavy,' she murmured breathlessly.

'Impossible.'

'Your legs...'

'Damn my legs.'

Holly gave up and began to kiss him back, and it was much later when he finally let her go and she sat on the edge of the bed, both his hands holding on tight to hers and her eyes shining with tears. 'I'm sorry, I'm so, so sorry,' she whispered tremblingly. 'I should never have

sent you away and then this wouldn't have happened.'
She glanced miserably at the cage.

'You did not send me away, *chérie*,' he murmured just
as softly. 'I chose to go, to give you a little time to come
to your senses. I did not intend to give up, not then, not
ever. And it was my decision to ride the bike on Christmas
Eve, not yours. The accident could have happened at any
time, any place.'

'But it didn't,' she whispered, tears starring her
eyelashes.

'No, it did not.' There was a faint shadow of the old
smile on his face. 'But it brought you to me, *n'est-ce pas*?
So this is good.'

'How can you say what has happened to you is good?'
she said shakily. 'You could have been killed, and your
poor legs…'

'My poor legs will heal,' he said drily, so much the old
Jacques she felt a stab of relief. 'Certainly in time for our
wedding. And I do not intend to die for a long, long time,
petite. I will not leave you, OK? We will make old bones
together.'

'Oh, Jacques.' She hadn't realised she was crying, the
tears slowly dripping down her cheeks, or that Jacques
had hit on the consuming fear which had eaten her up
ever since she had realised how much she loved him.
Everyone she had ever cared about had been taken from
her in the past; why should the future be any different?

'Old bones,' he repeated softly, his eyes smiling at her.
'Because you are going to marry me, are you not, *ma
chérie*? I do not know how you knew I was here, and now
you *are* here I do not care who brought you to me. I told
myself, once I could think again, that I would be strong
over this. I would not call you to my side and blackmail
your soft heart with pity. I would wait until my legs were

my own once more and then walk, tall and sound, into your life again and make you marry me. Now you are here I see this was foolishness. All pride vanishes the moment I see your face.'

'I don't believe that for a second,' she said huskily.

'Then you have much to learn about me,' he said, and smiled. The smile which always had the power to turn her world upside-down. 'And I of you, no doubt. But we will have much fun in the learning, yes? Kiss me, Holly,' he added thickly.

She placed her lips on his mouth gently but then, as his mouth sought hers and he kissed her with a fierce, possessive ardour, locking her against him, she felt her senses reel. His hands cupped her face as his mouth demanded greater intimacy, his desire reassuring her more than any words spoken by the medical profession could have done.

His hands moved over her upper torso, sliding under her top and touching her with sensual, intimate caresses which made her gasp against his lips for long, rainbow-coloured moments.

A sound from the corridor outside had her pulling away. '*Jacques*, someone's coming.' She sat up, smoothing her dishevelled hair away from her hot, flushed cheeks as she said, half laughing, 'What will they say if they find us making love in your hospital bed?'

'That I can get out of this damn place sooner than they thought, I hope.' And then his eyes darkened as they searched her face. 'Do you believe me now?' he said levelly. 'Enough to marry me as soon as I can walk out of here? That will do to start with, *petite*. The rest will come in time. Time that will convince you I love you and want you and need you more than life itself. Is the running over, Holly? Are you here to stay?'

She nodded wordlessly, incapable of uttering a sound but her eyes speaking out her love.

'We'll make our own world, *chérie*. Believe me on this too. A world in which our children will know how much they are wanted and loved, and that they will never have to go through what you did. Our world will be safe and secure and strong.'

A sudden explosion of sound from outside the hospital made them both stop and listen for a moment. 'Fireworks,' Holly said tremulously, her hands tight in his. 'It's New Year's Day, Jacques.'

'A new beginning,' he said softly, his heavy lids making her realise that whatever he said to the contrary he was exhausted. 'Ours to make of it what we will. And we'll make it good, *petite. Merveilleux! C'est extra!* You agree?'

'You'll have to teach me French.' Her throat was dry with the enormity of what she was committing to. 'I can't have our children speaking their father's language better than I do.'

'This is true.' A bronzed hand lifted to her face. 'But be it French or English I want you to speak out all your fears, *chérie*, whenever you need to. Understand me on this. However many times a day you need me I will be there for you. I promise you this. I love you.'

'And I love you,' she said shakily.

'Then that is all we need.'

CHAPTER TEN

JACQUES and Holly were married on the lawns of the château on a brilliantly beautiful and frosty February morning two months later.

The doctors had advised Jacques it would be several months and well into the spring before he could walk again. He'd cut the prediction by more than half, but then, as Lucy whispered to James during the short service, he had had everything to get well for, hadn't he?

Holly looked radiant in an ivory Duchesse satin dress with an organza and satin train, over which she wore a satin cloak trimmed with clouds of soft, floating feathers. She carried a small, simple bouquet of baby's breath, and her face, framed by the hood of the cloak, was luminous with love for the tall, dark man at her side.

Mrs Gibson, as outrageous as ever in a bright lemon fun-fur coat and matching hat, declared Holly the most beautiful bride she had ever seen and even had a little weep, which allowed the ever-hopeful Mr Bateman to put a comforting hand round her shoulders. He grinned like a Cheshire cat for the rest of the day.

The bridal pair honeymooned first in the Caribbean, followed by a month or two at the Great Barrier Reef. By the time they returned home to the château in the summer Jacques was walking as well as ever he had and Holly had the bloom of a truly loved and satisfied woman. Jacques told her a hundred times a day how much he loved her and the dark shadows were being banished for good.

Time passed, time in which Holly opened like a flower to the sun of Jacques's adoration, and when first a daughter and then a son was born to them they felt blessed.

And then, early in the morning that heralded their tenth wedding anniversary, when they lay locked in each other's arms in their enormous bed, Holly stirred in her husband's arms. The night had been one of love, the warm glow of which was still reflected in her voice when she said, 'Jacques, we're so very lucky.'

'I know it.' His voice was a deep, soothing rumble above her head.

'And it could have been so different.'

'No.' As she raised her face to stare into the beautiful amber eyes he was smiling. 'I would not have let it be,' he said softly. 'I would never have given up, *petite*. You know this.'

'I want more children, Jacques.' And then, as he went to reach for her as his smile widened, she said quickly, 'No, listen. I mean it. I want to foster children, little ones in need of love and care. Children who have been hurt by life, children like I was. I feel ready for this now. I want to give them a chance in life, as many children as they let us have, because...'

'What?' He touched her face with his hand, his eyes gentle. 'What, my love?'

'Because they might not all meet a Jacques later in life. They need us *now* because you were right. Love is all anyone needs to come out of the darkness into the light.'

'No more shadows, *petite*?'

'Not a single one.'

'Then you are right, it is time.'

And together they made it so.

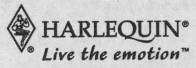

If you enjoyed what you just read,
then we've got an offer you can't resist!

Take 2 bestselling
love stories FREE!
Plus get a FREE surprise gift!

Clip this page and mail it to Harlequin Reader Service®

IN U.S.A.	**IN CANADA**
3010 Walden Ave.	P.O. Box 609
P.O. Box 1867	Fort Erie, Ontario
Buffalo, N.Y. 14240-1867	L2A 5X3

YES! Please send me 2 free Harlequin Presents® novels and my free surprise gift. After receiving them, if I don't wish to receive anymore, I can return the shipping statement marked cancel. If I don't cancel, I will receive 6 brand-new novels every month, before they're available in stores! In the U.S.A., bill me at the bargain price of $3.57 plus 25¢ shipping & handling per book and applicable sales tax, if any*. In Canada, bill me at the bargain price of $4.24 plus 25¢ shipping & handling per book and applicable taxes**. That's the complete price and a savings of at least 10% off the cover prices—what a great deal! I understand that accepting the 2 free books and gift places me under no obligation ever to buy any books. I can always return a shipment and cancel at any time. Even if I never buy another book from Harlequin, the 2 free books and gift are mine to keep forever.

106 HDN DNTZ
306 HDN DNT2

Name _____ (PLEASE PRINT)

Address _____ Apt.# _____

City _____ State/Prov. _____ Zip/Postal Code _____

* Terms and prices subject to change without notice. Sales tax applicable in N.Y.
** Canadian residents will be charged applicable provincial taxes and GST.
   All orders subject to approval. Offer limited to one per household and not valid to
   current Harlequin Presents® subscribers.
® are registered trademarks of Harlequin Enterprises Limited.

PRES02   ©2001 Harlequin Enterprises Limited

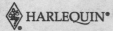

eHARLEQUIN.com

The eHarlequin.com online community is *the* place to share opinions, thoughts and feelings!

- Joining the community is easy, fun and **FREE!**
- Connect with **other romance fans** on our message boards.
- Meet your **favorite authors** without leaving home!
- **Share opinions** on books, movies, celebrities…and *more!*

Here's what our members say:

"I love the friendly and helpful atmosphere filled with support and humor."
—Texanna (eHarlequin.com member)

"Is this the place for me, or what? There is nothing I love more than 'talking' books, especially with fellow readers who are reading the same ones I am."
—Jo Ann (eHarlequin.com member)

Join today by visiting —— www.eHarlequin.com!

The world's bestselling romance series.

HARLEQUIN®
Presents~
Seduction and Passion Guaranteed!

Your dream ticket to the vacation of a lifetime!

Why not relax and allow Harlequin Presents® to whisk you away
to stunning international locations with our new miniseries…

*Where irresistible men and sophisticated women
surrender to seduction under the golden sun.*

Don't miss this opportunity to
experience glamorous lifestyles
and exotic settings in:

**Robyn Donald's
THE TEMPTRESS OF TARIKA BAY
on sale July, #2336**

**THE FRENCH COUNT'S MISTRESS
by Susan Stephens
on sale August, #2342**

**THE SPANIARD'S WOMAN
by Diana Hamilton
on sale September, #2346**

**THE ITALIAN MARRIAGE
by Kathryn Ross
on sale October, #2353**

FOREIGN AFFAIRS… A world full of passion!

**Pick up a Harlequin Presents® novel and you will enter a world
of spine-tingling passion and provocative, tantalizing romance!**

Available wherever Harlequin books are sold.

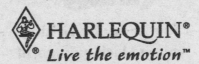

HARLEQUIN®
Live the emotion™

Visit us at www.eHarlequin.com

HPFAMA